KISS OF DEATH

The wind was howling through twisted tree tops, making the branches creak. Through blinding darkness she struggled up a hill, her hands slashed by the thorns which grew from tangled shrubs. The ground was so slick with dew that she pitched on her face, gulping in mud and dirt. But she could not slow down, for the pain was after her, bringing the fear and rage which lurk in maddened hearts. The pain was on the slope, chasing her like a beast. The pain was hunting her.

POINT CRIME

KISS OF DEATH

Peter Beere

Illustrated by David Wyatt

SCHOLASTIC

Scholastic Children's Books,
Scholastic Publications Ltd,
7–9 Pratt Street, London NW1 0AE, UK

Scholastic Inc.,
555 Broadway, New York, NY 10012-3999, USA

Scholastic Canada Ltd,
123 Newkirk Road, Richmond Hill,
Ontario, Canada L4C 3G5

Ashton Scholastic Pty Ltd,
P O Box 579, Gosford, New South Wales,
Australia

Ashton Scholastic Ltd,
Private Bag 92801, Penrose, Auckland,
New Zealand

First published by Scholastic Publications Ltd, 1994

Copyright © Peter Beere, 1994

ISBN 0 590 55583 9

Typeset by TW Typesetting, Midsomer Norton, Avon
Printed by Cox & Wyman Ltd, Reading, Berks

10 9 8 7 6 5 4 3 2 1

Often the fear of one evil leads us into a worse.

Nicholas Boileau

Prologue

On the day that David went away to begin his media studies course at Leeds University, he and Sadie made a solemn vow that they would write to each other every day, no matter what happened. They made it seriously, as many vows are made. They swore it on their lives, crossed it through on their hearts. But like a lot of vows it became hard to keep when life got in the way. David replied to Sadie's letters until things intervened. His letters slowed down from a flood to a trickle, then a drop, and then the flow ran out.

Sadie herself kept writing for some weeks after that, but it was difficult to keep her side of the bargain when she received nothing back. It's hard to stay in love when the object of your love keeps avoiding you.

So she, too, stopped writing, not because she wanted to, but because it was too painful to keep banging her head against a wall . . .

1

"I'm surprised he wrote to you for that long," said Sadie's step-sister. "He never liked you much."

They were in the cluttered kitchen, where Sadie was preparing a meal under the withering gaze of the person she most loathed – her step-sister, Eleanor.

"And how would you know? You don't know anything."

The wither became a smirk: Eleanor was very good at that. Of all her expressions her superior smirking one was the most refined of all.

She said, "I think you're pitiful."

"Why don't you give it a break?"

"I can't," said Eleanor. "I get so much from it. Of all the people I've ever known, you are, beyond a doubt, quite the *most* pitiful. I really love it, watching you writhe and squirm. It really cheers me up to see you so depressed. But I wouldn't want you to get the wrong idea and think I don't care – no, quite the opposite. In fact, I've brought you a present, Sadie, I found it in the fields . . ." Eleanor held her hands out, to reveal a dead blackbird. Its body was quite stiff; blood showed across its chest.

"Get that thing out of here!" Sadie yelled. "I'm trying to cook a meal."

"I know you like blackbirds," Eleanor continued. "I read it in your red book."

"What are you talking about?"

"That book hidden under your bed. Your little 'special' book. Your book of precious thoughts—"

"That's a private book!" Sadie cried. "You're not to look at it!"

"Oh, my!" said Eleanor. "And there's me snooping around. Looking under your bed, peeking through all your drawers. Finding out all your plans, reading your hopes and dreams, reading your love letters . . ."

Sadie snatched up a courgette and hacked it into chunks. "Why are you so horrible?"

"I suppose I'm just made that way." Eleanor threw the blackbird down. "I don't think it's wrong to pry into the thoughts of someone as pitiful as you. It's like reading a child's dreams—"

"Just keep away from my things!"

"Or what? What will you do?" Eleanor asked brazenly. "Will you try to beat me up? Are you going to tell your dad?"

"I don't know what I'll do." Sadie was almost rigid with anger and despair. Ever since Eleanor arrived in the house she had been goading her, pushing her to the edge, undermining her life.

And it was so one-sided; Sadie just couldn't compete. She would have to toughen up, or her step-sister would trample all over her.

There was a ferocious rivalry between the girls, and so far Eleanor was winning hands down. Unless Sadie found a way to halt her in her stride, it would all be over soon.

"This is the second bird I've dug up today. The other was shot, too – do you see the hole in it? I wondered if perhaps it was you, going out with a gun and shooting helpless things."

Sadie said, "I don't kill anything."

"But you've got the Kiss of Death. Everything you've ever touched has died or disappeared. Your boyfriend disappeared – even your mother died to get away from you. Why can't you realize that you're just a problem now? No one wants you around. Why don't you disappear too? Leave the rest of us in peace so that we can settle down to living normally."

"Why are you trying to do this?" Sadie looked

into two dead eyes, eyes cold as pale sapphires half-buried in the snow. "Are you trying to take my place?"

"What do you think you've got that I could ever want?"

"I've got my father."

Eleanor laughed. "I'm not so sure. Have you seen the way he's been looking at you these last few weeks? I think he's got some doubts – though when he looks at me he's overcome with love. It's my 'tragic history'."

Sadie snorted bitterly, and threw a saucepan down. It bounced back off the stove, and rolled across the floor. "What tragic history?"

"My father's cruelty," Eleanor said with mocking eyes. "He wasn't a very *nice* man, and your father feels the guilt my father should have felt, so he loves me all the more. He's trying to patch up my soul, giving me all the love I never had before. And I'm so nice to *him*, too – how much love can he have left to give to you, Sadie? Not very much, I think."

"You're being ridiculous!" But Sadie chilled inside, hearing those ominous words.

"I just want what's mine. And what I want is this." Eleanor's eyes embraced the room. "I want the whole of it: your father and the house and every last drop of love. I've always been denied it, and I think I'd kill for it now—"

"You're mad," Sadie whispered, clutching the knife again. There was nothing left to chop, but she felt more secure holding it in her hand. "Why don't you go and look for more dead blackbirds? That's just your style!"

"You don't know the half of it!"

Eleanor walked out laughing, while Sadie scooped the bird from the kitchen floor and dropped it into a bin.

Only when the soft laughter had died away did she put down the knife.

2

BELOVED MARGARET ROSS
DEVOTED WIFE TO JOHN
MOTHER OF SADIE

The letters glinted in the sharp graveyard light, shining back at the sun like messages to God. But they didn't begin to scratch the surface of the loss contained within the grave. They were never meant to, for no words can plumb that pain. No phrase can begin to *hint* at such anguish and loss. We use the quietest voice to speak the loudest words, knowing they can't be heard . . .

Sadie rubbed at the black tombstone with a soft yellow cloth, smoothing away a stain. She put some red carnations down and took the dead ones out. She said, "I miss you, Mum. I'm having a really hard time. I wish that you were here to tell me what to do. I want to sit and cry." She flicked her long hair back as she knelt down on the stones. "I feel so lonely sometimes, I wish that I could die. I want to be with you. I want to hold your hand. I need you to comfort me."

She remembered a phrase of Eleanor's – that death is "just a dream". It's not a dream at all – it's the greatest truth. It lasts for ever and can never be reversed.

She started crying, because there was no hope of her mum coming back to help her.

"Is that your mother?"

Sadie's damp eyes glanced up. She nodded. "Yes, it is."

A youth looked down at her with startling blue eyes. He said, "Mine's over there, in the shadow by the wall. My father disappeared up north to Birmingham."

"I'm sorry," Sadie said.

The youth knelt beside her. "I come to talk to her."

"I talk to my mum, too."

"But she never answers me."

"Sometimes I think mine does."

"Then you're lucky," the youth whispered. "I can't hear anything at all."

He flicked his dark hair back and squinted at the sun. He said, "But I keep on coming, just in case she ever does. My name's Tony, by the way. Tony Stern."

"My name's Sadie Ross."

"Nice to meet you, Sadie." He remained kneeling beside her, staring at her mother's grave.

"Nice head-stone," he remarked.

"It never seems like much."

"They never do," he said. "People who write too much – they don't know what to say."

Then he picked a flower out of the bunch in his own hand, and laid it on the grave beside the carnations.

"One more can't go amiss," he said. "The dead like flowers. It makes them think of life."

"Where did you go this afternoon?"

"I went to the cemetery," she told her father.

"We were all wondering," he said. "We were supposed to go out for lunch."

"I forgot," Sadie murmured. "But no doubt I wasn't missed."

"Why do you talk like that?"

"Because that's the way I feel. I don't like Melanie." Sadie tossed her hair back, watching her father's eyes. They had been through this before, arguing over his new wife. But this time they didn't row – he just looked forlorn. He looked hurt.

"Why do you keep on with this? Why can't you let it rest?"

"It's not a game, you know. They're trying to squeeze me out."

"That's absolute rot!" Her father rubbed his hair. His eyes looked sad and lost.

Sadie couldn't help him – he had made his choice. It was up to him to see the truth of what was going on. She could talk until she was blue in the face, but he would never see how evil Eleanor was.

She pushed roughly past him and grabbed her mountain bike. She wheeled it out of the hall and cycled down the drive, heading for the hills, where she could be alone.

3

Sadie tugged her books out of a bottom drawer. A new school year had begun.

She gazed into the mirror and saw that she was getting thinner. The constant, gnawing strain was taking a toll on her.

There were shadows around her eyes, and her hair looked lank and thin. It probably wasn't as bad as she thought, but was still noticeable. Not only was Eleanor shredding her nerves, she was beginning to wipe the looks from her face.

Sadie set off for school, feeling that she looked a mess and that it was all Eleanor's fault. She wasn't cheered by the thought that Eleanor herself would be at her school this year. She hoped she wouldn't be cleverer than her or make better friends. She hoped the entire school would turn its back on her. But somehow Eleanor seemed to have a way about her that made people flock to her.

That was all Sadie needed: to see her step-sister become the most popular girl in the school, friend to each passing soul. She would probably get Sadie expelled. Nothing Eleanor did would surprise her any more.

What was it with some people that they could waltz through life while others tried so hard and got nowhere fast? Did God like them the best, or was it down to chance, just the luck of the draw?

"What are you thinking about?"

"Oh! hi, Karen. Nothing much. Just the bane of my life."

"Who's that then? Tracey?" Karen fell into step beside Sadie.

"Oh, gosh! I'd forgotten about her. No, Eleanor the Beast. Do you know they've moved in now? They got married in July."

"You never told me."

"It wasn't much of a do. Only the four of us, and two friends as witnesses. I kept hoping it wouldn't come off, that someone would stand up and shout '*Hold everything!*' But they never did," Sadie said sorrowfully. "It all just went ahead, and we went out for lunch. And now she's in the house, rooting through my things and stealing half my clothes."

"So you still don't like her?"

"That's putting it generously. I wish Eleanor would die. I'd dance on her grave."

"She seemed okay to me."

"You only met her once. You don't have to live with her."

Sadie and Karen slowed down at the sight of trouble ahead. A group of the sixth-form girls had cornered Martin Kemp. Martin was the kind of youth who attracted trouble. He had that sort of face.

He was a fairly quiet boy, and good looking in a way, but he had made one big mistake: he had shot his neighbour's cats. It had made the newspapers, Martin had been sent for "therapy", and the doctor he saw happened to be Tracey Scott's dad. Tracey was cool and chic; Tracey ruled half the school; Tracey was a pain in the neck.

"So how's the fruitcake then?"

"You should never have found that out. You shouldn't have told anyone."

"What? That we've got a psycho parading in our midst?" Tracey's laugh snorted out and echoed around the school. "I ought to check your notes."

"This isn't right, Tracey."

"As if I care," she said. Tracey was a callous girl who fed off others' woes. She was also, somewhat maddeningly, stunningly good looking, and though beauty may be only skin-deep, that fact can easily be overlooked. Every boy in the school, plus half the teachers, collapsed at Tracey's feet.

"No," Tracey went on, "I really think we have to be aware of this: if you start off with a cat, your next most logical step is, what? A cow? A horse? And before you know it, you're running amok – a complete psychopath!"

"That isn't fair, Tracey," Martin said, looking round as if he wished the ground would open up and swallow him. "It's not like that at all. You shouldn't read my notes – they're confidential."

Tracey looked flabbergasted. "Oh, *confidential*, is it?" she said, raising a laugh. "You mean we're not supposed to know that you're a lunatic?"

"Just pack it in, Tracey."

"Yes, pack it in, Tracey," Sadie said irritably. "You're always picking on him. Just leave Martin alone."

"Oh, my! A heroine has come rushing to your aid. It's Sadie Ross," Tracey snarled. The group of friends around her sneered. Wherever Tracey went she attracted hangers-on.

"It's so childish to keep going on like this," Sadie continued.

"Oh, of course *you're* so mature, aren't you?"

"Just walk away, Martin. She isn't worth your time. Look out your other friends."

Martin Kemp shot Sadie a grateful look as he slipped out of the scene. "Thanks very much,

Sadie," he said before he disappeared.

"He's never done anything to you; why can't you leave him alone?"

"Because he's a psychopath."

It didn't seem worth trying to talk things through – reasoning with Tracey Scott was like hammering at a brick wall. So Sadie turned away, with Karen at her side.

"You're just so saintly," Tracey sneered, "it almost brings a tear—"

"Oh, knock it on the head!" Sadie snapped, walking off. This was a really great start to the new school year: carrying on where things left off.

As Karen peeled away to talk to some of their other friends, Martin approached Sadie.

"Thanks for sticking up for me."

"You shouldn't need my support. You know what Tracey's like; why don't you keep out of her way?"

"I don't know," Martin said. He wasn't the brightest of souls, and thoughts came ponderously. "I just keep walking into things. I look before I leap."

"You mean the other way round."

"Something like that," he said. "I can't think fast enough; I can't—"

"I know," Sadie said. "Forget it." She smiled.

He smiled back awkwardly. "I just want you to know, if you ever need *my* help—"

"I'll be sure to let you know."

Sadie touched him on the arm, then continued on her way as the bell rang in the school.

4

Sadie stood in the doorway to her classroom and watched her world cave in. Her love letters from Dave, her secret diary – all were on open display, pinned up on the walls. Her classmates were having the time of their lives comparing titbits here with bits of gossip there, as they rushed around, tracking down every stage of her doomed love affair.

In their midst sat the cold-eyed Eleanor, lapping it all up. Never in her wildest dreams could she have thought she would create such a stir on her first day at school.

"Hey, Sadie!" she cried, as Sadie stalled outside. "Some of your writing's blurred – come and read it to us!"

Sadie's world crashed around her with a sound like thunder in her heart. She shot in, and frantically snatched all the pages up, then she ran out of the room, with the thunder echoing in her ears. The first thing she saw outside was the approaching figure of Martin Kemp, clutching still more of her "thoughts".

"They're all over the school," he said. "I've pulled most of them down—"

Sadie was too shocked to speak as she grabbed them from his hands.

"They were on the main notice board. They were over all the walls. Did you put them there?" he asked.

"*Martin, are you crazy?*" she almost screamed at him. "Who do you think I am? Do you think I *want* them to read this stuff? What do you think – Oh, Martin, what am I going to do?"

"I don't know," Martin replied, flushing with embarrassment at being faced by Sadie's pain. "I'll sort things out—"

"How *can* you sort things out?"

She fled from the school and ran all the way home, laughter ringing in her ears.

Alone in her room Sadie curled up on her bed, shaking with grief and rage. The humiliation of this day would live with her for the rest of her life; she would never live it down. How could she show her face again? How could she ever look her class-mates in the eyes? They would hoot with laughter, they would never let it drop. Over and over again they would be quoting lines at her. They would say *"Remember this? How you said you'd die if he ever left you?"*

How could she face them? How could she face herself? How could she ever again hold her head up in this town?

It hardly registered when Melanie came into her room and put her soft, warm hands on her ruffled hair. "What is it, Sade?" she said.

Sadie squirmed away from her. "I want to die," she said.

She felt sick inside. She didn't think she had any strength left to combat Eleanor's wickedness. Her step-sister was a great spider, gloating inside her web.

"Eleanor's trying to destroy me. She's trying to grind me down."

"Don't be stupid—"

"It's true," Sadie muttered.

Her father came in. He had a day off work. Now everyone could see her shame.

"What's going on?" he asked.

"For some reason she thinks Eleanor's got it in for her." Melanie rose from the bed and looked help-lessly at Sadie's father. "I don't know what she's talking about; she won't say any more than that."

Sadie's father frowned, not sure how to react.

"It's the first day back at school. Is this how it's going to be for the whole of your last year?"

Sadie glared up at him. "What do you think I am? Do you think I'm making this up? That girl's after me – she's trying to take your love and make a fool of me."

"Don't be stupid—"

"That's just what Melanie said!" She stared at her father and Melanie, and felt that their eyes were looking right through her. She could sense an awful void between herself and her dad. "I'm not an idiot!"

"I know," her father said. "Maybe we've pushed too hard. There's been a lot of change – maybe you need more time to come to terms with it."

"I don't need time!" she screamed. "Don't you understand? Eleanor's after me!"

"Your mother's death, Sadie – it was hard for both of us. You've been through this before – the nightmares—"

"I still get them!" she cried. "I get the nightmares, I get the paranoia! I get this stupid girl trying to take my place! And I don't get any help – nobody talks to *me*. Nobody takes my side!"

"Maybe if we see a doctor – get some professional help—"

"The only help I need is to get rid of Eleanor!"

Sadie's eyes blurred with tears. She felt them flood her cheeks and drip on to her hands.

5

"**D**escribe your dreams to me. Tell me about the birds," said the psychiatrist.

Sadie stared hard at her, trying to read her thoughts. She had never been this close to a psychiatrist before. What did the woman really think? Did she think Sadie was mad? "What?" she said, after a while.

"I said, your dreams, Sadie. Describe your dreams to me." Mrs Cox gave a smile, designed to put her at her ease.

It didn't really work. Sadie felt like a worm under a microscope.

"I, erm – have nightmares," she started clumsily. "Nightmares that wake me up – they jerk me out of sleep."

"Nightmares about the birds?"

"Yes, among other things. But mostly birds," she said.

Mrs Cox nodded, and fumbled with her pen. It dropped out of her hand and rolled across the desk, finally coming to rest against a green leather blotting pad. As she picked it up again she gave another smile, this time more genuine, and Sadie's eyes smiled back. Mrs Cox said, "That's not supposed to happen. I'm supposed to be in control." She put the pen away.

Uncrossing her knotted legs, Sadie said, "It's the birds that usually start the dreams. The birds are screaming, because their wings have been torn off. They're lying on the ground, heaped up like autumn leaves. I can't step over them, and as I try to walk I keep on crushing them. That's part of the reason they're screaming – because I'm crushing them. I can feel their bones snap like twigs under my feet. They're trying to crawl away, trailing their broken legs, and I keep crushing them."

"Where do you think this place is, Sadie?"

"I don't know. It might be Hell. There are a million rooms filled with screaming birds. The rooms are black as night, and there's a smell in the air like burning sulphur. Nothing seems to be in the place except the tortured birds, until I come to a huge black door at the end of a long passage. There's a blackened skull on the door, and I know that behind that door is the throne room of Death."

"Have you ever entered the room?" asked the psychiatrist.

"I do now," Sadie said, in a soft, low voice. "At first I used to wake up each time I reached the door, but now I lift the latch and the door swings slowly back. Almost against my will I'm drawn into the room, one footstep at a time. It's very dark inside, but then a flame appears – it comes from a brand fixed to the wall. It fills the room with flickering light and shadows."

The room became almost silent as the psychiatrist stared into Sadie's dark eyes as if half-mesmerized. Or perhaps she mesmerized Sadie herself to draw her story out. Maybe it was both of these things.

"Have you ever seen Death?"

"I see him all the time. He's standing by the throne. The throne is empty, waiting for me. He's wearing a long dark grey cloak, and when he holds out his arm it slips back from his hand. All the dying birds have been trying to warn me not to go into the room, but Death draws me towards the throne. The birds crawl after me, begging me to turn back, but I still go on to him. Death wants to touch me and stop my heart, and make me as dead as him, so that I'll stay for ever. He wants to take my soul and give it wings, and then rip holes in it."

"Why should he want to do this?" the young psychiatrist asked.

"To make me lose all hope and give in to him. He took my mother's life, but she wasn't enough, so now he's coming for me."

Mrs Cox stared hard at her. "How did your mother die?"

"She had a heart attack and collapsed in the street. It must have been very quick, because she had already gone by the time an ambulance arrived."

"And were you with her when she died?"

"We were on a shopping trip. We had just come out of Boots. There was a bird trapped in the roof of the new shopping arcade. It looked like a jackdaw."

Mrs Cox said, "So you think it's significant that you see birds in your dreams?"

"I think they're harbingers – warnings of deaths to come. And I see them all the time; it seems everywhere I go these days I see flocks of black-birds . . ."

"So now they've got you, too," Eleanor said that stormy night. "Another fruitcake."

She was standing in the darkness of Sadie's quiet bedroom. She had a long white sweatshirt on, which lent her a spectral look. She was combing her thick, dark hair with Sadie's hair brush. She was wearing Sadie's perfume.

She started laughing as she looked down at Sadie. It was a callous laugh, with no trace of humour present. Then she slipped out of the room, but her laughter lingered on.

6

"How do you feel today?"

"Not too bad," Sadie said, as her father bent to touch her face.

"I've brought you some magazines," he said. "And Lucozade."

"I always get Lucozade when I'm ill."

"You're not ill," he murmured. "You've just been under stress. You need to rest for a while."

She said, "I don't want to rest; I want to go outside."

She tossed the covers back, but her father made her stay in bed. "It's raining cats and dogs out there. You'll not miss anything by staying here in bed."

Sadie asked, "Am I going crazy?"

"Don't be ridiculous. You're just a very stubborn girl who refuses to stay in bed."

"Then I must be a lot like Mum. You said she was stubborn, too."

Her father nodded. "Yes, she was."

"Am I a lot like her?" asked Sadie.

"Yes, you are. Every time I look at you I can see your mother there." Her father sat on the bed. He pulled the covers up, and adjusted them round her chin. He said, "You've got the same eyes, and the same slant to your jaw. Sometimes I think it's her when I hear your voice in the distance. If you're laughing in the lane I think she's coming home, and she's forgotten the car."

Sadie said, "Do you still think of her?"

"I think of her all the time." Her father's eyes were soft and grey. "I think of her every day. There's not an hour goes by when I don't wonder where she is now."

"I never knew that."

"It's hard to talk about."

"Maybe we should have talked."

"Maybe we should at that. Some things just hurt so much we try to shut them out, like they're our secret thoughts. They seem too personal – hard to put into words. It's as if we're the only ones who'll never understand. And it's only us who'll know how much we hurt inside, so we keep it to ourselves."

"That can't be right, though."

"No, Sade, it isn't right. We should have talked before instead of clamming up. We went off in different directions because we were so involved in struggling with ourselves."

"It really hurt me—"

"I know. It hurt me, too. But Mum wouldn't have died if there'd been some other way. She would have given the world to have just one more day—"

"I never said goodbye!"

That was what really hurt Sadie; the fact that she'd never had the chance to say one last goodbye, or tell her mother how much she loved her. She had spent their last half hour together complaining that the shops were out of her lipstick.

What a stupid thing to talk about when her mother was about to die! If only she'd been warned, she could have talked about something else . . .

Her father said, "Your mother knew. Your mother always knew. She was a wise woman."

Sadie said, "If I got the chance again I'd tell her everything!"

"I know," her father said. "So would I. Sometimes we leave these things too late."

"It's not going to happen to us?"

"No, Sade." Her father smiled.

*   *   *

"You had another dream?"

"It was the worst one I've ever had. I woke up drenched with sweat."

Mrs Cox nodded. "When we're under stress, dreams can reflect our fears. They'll show your sense of loneliness, what you see as rejection, and confusion at your mother's death."

She tapped her gold pen and glanced down at her hands. Her well-cropped auburn hair curled about her face. In the bright sunlight it had a coppery tint, as though lit by fire. "Why do *you* think you have such powerful dreams?"

"I don't know," Sadie said. "I suppose because of what you said. And also because of Eleanor. I feel guilty about her, though I don't know why I should."

Mrs Cox said, "You don't really view her as part of the family yet?"

"Well, she isn't," Sadie said. "She's come in from outside."

"But you can accept Melanie more, because you don't see her as a direct threat to your father's love for you?"

Sadie said, "Don't ask me. I'm not the psychiatrist."

"I'm just curious as to whether you feel differently about the two of them. They've both come from outside, but it seems to be Eleanor who's causing you problems."

"That's because she's a little witch who's trying to take my place!" Sadie whipped her gaze away to stare out at the lawns. They were like a deep green tide rolling towards the room. She wished she was outside; she wished she wasn't in here facing this interrogation.

"Why are you defending her?" she asked after a pause.

"I'm not," said Mrs Cox. "Though you're a little sensitive whenever she's mentioned." She gave a hint of a smile to show that this was irony, and she wasn't having a go at her. "She's struggling too, you know."

"Then let *her* come to you." Sadie was watching a robin on the lawn. Two squawking magpies flew down and it fluttered away. "She hates me too, you know."

"You both have the same fears. You're frightened of losing your dad; she'll be scared of losing her mum. You're both struggling to come to terms with the altered circumstances you've been thrust into."

"'Thrust' is the right word," Sadie said bitterly. "We didn't have any choice in the matter; we were just thrown together."

"And if you had a choice, would you pick Eleanor to be one of your friends?"

"I doubt it," said Sadie. "She's just another one of the problems I've got. I'll sort them out myself."

She couldn't see much help coming from Mrs Cox.

7

She read the ad several times, but she still couldn't believe it was meant for her. It was in the local newspaper, among the personal ads. It said: *Would Sadie Ross like to meet Tony Stern?* It gave a box number, and added: *Please reply.*

Are you kidding? Sadie thought. Guys didn't write to you like that, through newspapers. Guys talked to you at school, or met you at a dance. They met you in the street when you were with all your friends – not in a cemetery.

Would she like to meet him? Well, she'd already met him once, and yes, he was pretty cute but – I don't know, she thought. An ad in the newspaper – and it was right next to the "Lonely Hearts". She wasn't that lonely.

How lonely did you have to be, though, to go and meet someone? It wasn't really as if he was a stranger to her. It was just – what other way could he find of getting in touch? He could have tried the phone directory . . .

Would she like to meet him? I don't know, Sadie thought. This is a bit too weird, like – what was that old film? The one with Trevor Howard, set in a railway station? Yes, *Brief Encounter*.

Was that what it was? A momentary thing that somehow lingered on, took root, and then blossomed? Could this be the start of the greatest love of all? Somehow Sadie doubted it.

On the other hand, there was something quite sweet about his placing an ad in the hope that she would pick it up. Maybe he was very shy, and didn't want to phone in case she turned him down. Perhaps he was sitting there even at this moment, racked with torment and doubt, wondering whether he had been wise or was about to get slapped down. Maybe all his friends would see what he was doing and mock his small designs. Sadie could feel a mild sense of panic, as if this half-known boy had somehow invaded her private life.

She could still remember him clearly: the darkness of his hair, the sparkle of his blue eyes, the way he tugged at his lower lip . . .

Maybe he really *was* shy, and the only time he could talk was when he felt secure, close by his mother's grave. The chances of meeting her again that way were really very slim, so he'd placed the ad.

"What are you looking at?" said Eleanor.

"Nothing," Sadie said, as she screwed the paper up and stuffed it into a bin.

But his name stuck in her mind. So did the box number. In case she needed it.

"A penny for your thoughts."

"A penny isn't enough to buy my thoughts, Martin."

Sadie flicked her hair back, as she watched Martin approach. She was sitting on a bench at the side of the River Trent. It ran straight through the town, swirling contentedly, gurgling at the banks. In the winter it could roar through, but at the moment it was low, and a group of snow-white swans were up-ending for food. They were pulling up clumps of weed in which small molluscs lurked, having nightmares about swans.

"Are you looking at the swans?" Martin sat on the wooden bench, leaving a small gap between them.

Sadie didn't mind Martin, though some people found him weird. Maybe it wasn't Martin himself, more the friends he kept, notably the two Cope brothers. Maurice and Stephen Cope were the low-spots of the town, and any friend of theirs was probably best left alone. It sometimes seemed to Sadie, though, that Martin wasn't their friend – they just made him think he was.

"I've been watching them feeding," she said.

Martin said, "It's a wonder they don't drown. They sometimes seem to hold their heads under the water for hours."

She said, "The swans don't drown because they don't think they will."

"That's very philosophical." Martin spoke gravely, but she thought he was teasing her, and it rather cheered her up to see him in that light. Usually he was so intense he could be depressing.

"I was going into town," he said.

"I'm just on my way."

"I heard you haven't been well." He threw a stone at the metal railings which stood at the edge of the park, above the river bank. The railings were thin and low, more of a gesture than a serious obstacle.

Sadie said, "It was nothing. I had a couple of days in bed."

"I thought your step-sister might have been getting you down." He threw another stone, and this one *pinged* away off the bright lower rail.

"No more than usual. She always gets me down."

"I can imagine," Martin said. "She's not a nice person." He looked inside his jacket and found a packet of mints. He offered one to her. "We could sort her out if you like."

"Who could?"

"Me and Maurice." Martin looked down awkwardly, at the short, litter-strewn grass. "Tell her to leave you alone."

"I can fight my own battles."

"I was looking for some way to help. It isn't much fun when people are picking on you. I'm kind of an expert there, knowing what bullying's like. Sometimes you don't know what to do, and you need somebody else to bale you out of it." He still looked awkward, but now he was looking at her. "I really like you, Sade; I'd like to be able to help."

"Well, it's very sweet of you," she said, "but I'm okay. I can handle Eleanor."

"I *really* like you," he went on, blushing now, but convinced that having gone this far he ought to see it through. "I like you as a friend, and as the kind of girl I'd like to go out with."

"I like you too, Martin," she said. "But not that way. It's nice to have a friend who's just . . ." She gave a shrug. "Someone who's always around but doesn't threaten you. Do you know what I mean?"

He shrugged. "I suppose so," he murmured. He picked up another stone and held it in his hand.

"It's very sweet of you."

"But you don't want to go on a date?" This time he threw the stone.

Sadie watched it go sailing out past the metal railings and down in the mud at the edge of the brown river. "I've got a lot on my mind. A lot of things to do."

"It's okay," Martin said. "A lot of the boys like you. I suppose you must know that."

"I've never thought of it," she said, watching the swans. "I suppose most people don't."

"*I* never have," he said. "*I've* never thought that way."

After a time he left her and wandered into town.

"Who's that you're looking at?"

"Martin Kemp," Sadie said. "I've just been talking to him."

She shuffled sideways as Karen joined her on the bench. They were supposed to have met in town, but Karen hadn't turned up. Her bus had been delayed and she'd had to get a lift from a neighbour with a van.

"He really likes you. He's got a crush on you."

"He just offered me the chance to have Eleanor beaten up."

"Are you going to take it up?"

"What do you think?" Sadie said. "She isn't *that* awful."

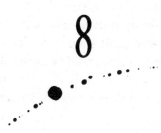

8

Someone who *was* awful was the creepy Maurice Cope, a local hooligan. He and his brother were two petty criminals from a family rife with them. The Copes were notorious for being at the heart of most of the trouble in the town.

The two boys were obnoxious in several different ways, not least of which was their belief in their attractiveness to girls. They were as attractive as dead ducks, but that never seemed to interfere with their misguided view of themselves.

"Hi, Sade!" Maurice appeared with his younger brother in tow, as she waited for a bus. "What are you doing here, then?"

"I'm waiting for a bus."

"Are you going into town?" Maurice flicked his long hair back. It had been of more use where it was, helping to hide the spots which dotted his forehead. "We're going there ourselves," he said. "Do you want to come with us?"

"No, thanks."

Maurice gave a shrug, and his leather jacket creaked. He thought it made him look tough, but it was a size too big, and almost fell off him. "Yeah, we're going to a party. Do you want to come along?"

"I'm going to meet someone," she muttered, staring hard at the empty street ahead, wishing her bus would come, wishing they'd disappear, hating the smell of them.

"Someone better than us?" he asked.

"Who isn't better than you?"

"What did she say, Maurice?" asked Stephen.

"I don't know." Maurice leaned closer to her. "What did you say, Sadie?"

"I said I'm going out with Karen."

"Oh, the fat girl?" he said. "Well, we could come along."

"No thanks. And anyway, you've got your own party."

"We could go there afterwards. What's wrong with you, Sadie? Don't you like me and Steve?"

Maurice offered her his "winning" look, which might have won a prize in an ugly-mug contest, but wasn't about to win her.

He said, "We're pretty cute."

"I'm sure."

He pulled a face. "Aw, come, on, what's the matter with you?" He leaned forward and tried to take her arm.

Sadie pulled away from him, saying, "Get off, will you?" She had been through this before; they were always trying to handle her, trying to chat her up. "Leave me alone, will you?"

"Why are you always so stuck up?"

"I'm not stuck up," she said. "I don't like being abused."

"That's not abuse," he said. "You don't know real abuse. You haven't seen it yet."

He never got a chance to demonstrate because a bus arrived and Sadie dived inside, not caring where it went. The youths stayed in the street, cat-calling after her as the green bus disappeared.

9

Sadie sat at the back of the bus, trying to forget the Cope brothers. They were a constant problem, people like Maurice and Steve – the kind of murky things you find at the bottom of a stagnant pond.

Fumbling in her coat for a handkerchief, she found a little scrap of paper on which she had jotted down a name. It was the name of "Tony", the boy from the cemetery, the boy who had placed the ad hoping to meet Sadie. It all seemed a world away from the technique of the Copes, and a not unattractive one.

At least he hadn't lunged at her the way Maurice had, nor hooted like a fool as her bus pulled down the street. He didn't strut around brandishing his pockmarked face like some kind of badge of war.

Maybe there were still some nice guys out there amongst the dross; the kind of boys who knew how to behave themselves. Sadie could really do with a friend now that David had gone. She had such love inside.

"Who's that you're writing to?"

"No one," Sadie replied, as Eleanor entered the room.

"You've got a pad there—"

"I'm just writing down some notes. Some things I need for school." Sadie sat on the pad. The last thing she needed was to have her step-sister butting in with advice.

Eleanor watched her suspiciously. "Do you mean like proper friends? Or maybe a better brain so that you don't keep flunking art?"

"You're such a witty girl," Sadie said sarcastically. "You really hit the mark."

Eleanor sat down shrugging, and rested her long legs across the coffee table on which Sadie had been trying to write. She looked at her fingernails and said almost casually, "So you met Maurice Cope? He really likes you."

"Do me a favour!" Sadie said.

"You're just playing hard to get – I know you like him too. In fact, I told him that this very afternoon. I said you've got the hots for him."

"What did you tell him that for?" said Sadie, aghast. "Those lies of yours will get you into trouble one day."

"I don't think so," Eleanor purred, "because I'm so good at it. They'll get *you* into trouble, though." She gave Sadie a sweet smile, the kind of sickly smile a cat might give a mouse in the moment before it strikes. "I spread it all round school that you and Maurice Cope are quite an item. It caused some raised eyebrows until I filled them in on all the sordid things you two get up to."

"Won't you give up ruining me?"

"Oh, no, there's still some way to go yet," Eleanor said. She swung her legs down and floated from the chair, looking as if butter wouldn't melt in her small, rosebud mouth. "It's just so delightful to watch you disappear beneath the weight of lies that I'm heaping on you. It's really quite a task to break down all the trust that your friends put in you."

She left the room laughing, tossing her thick black hair. She left the door open, so that Sadie could hear her joy. She ran out to the lawn, spreading her long thin arms, as if to embrace the world . . .

10

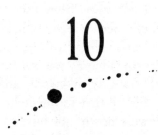

Ignoring Eleanor, Sadie finished off her note, then went out and posted it. She didn't want to go home while Eleanor was there, nor did she want to go into town, in case she met Maurice Cope. In fact, thanks to Eleanor, there weren't many places she liked to go now.

One spot was her own, though: Eleanor had no reason at all ever to go to the cemetery. It was Sadie's last refuge in an increasingly hostile world.

Sunshine broke through the clouds as Sadie walked up the drive of brown and red gravel. A hearse stood purring there, as if it could hardly wait to unload its coffin and race back into town. A group of mourners stood near, uncertain what to say and unsure where to stand. As Sadie walked past them she recognized someone; the man who brought the logs for the Aga in the kitchen. He gave her a wistful smile and Sadie nodded back. His father had just died.

As Sadie turned away from the scene into an avenue of spindly trees which rattled in the wind, she saw the distant shape of the boy who had placed the ad, crouching by his mother's grave. He made her feel strangely awkward, and she turned to walk away, but at that moment he spotted her. He put his flowers down and hurried over to her. "I wrote you a note," he said.

Sadie said, "I noticed. I've just written back to you."

"You have?" His blue eyes shone. "What did you write?" he asked.

"You'll have to wait and see."

"No, tell me now," he said, shaking with nervousness. "I can't stand the tension; I've been waiting for six days. Every day I phoned the shop to see if you'd replied. Oddly enough, two people had replied, but neither one was you. They were just lonely hearts."

Sadie said, "I agreed to meet you."

"You did? That's wonderful! I mean – we've saved some time—"

"I could have saved a stamp."

He laughed. "I couldn't stop – I kept seeing

your face in my mind. I've never felt like that."

Sadie looked away, smiling and blushing, not sure of what to say. His joy at her reply was all too plain to see.

"You're just so gorgeous – I didn't know what to say." Words were spilling out of him. "It must be fate," he said. "I think you are the most beautiful girl I've ever seen—"

"You can't have seen many."

"No, I've seen loads," he said. "Absolutely millions."

He seemed so happy, joy was bubbling out of him.

"You must be crazy if you don't think that!" he cried. "Just look at a mirror – you'll see what I mean."

"You're very kind," she said.

"That's not kindness," he said. "That's just the truth. I can't believe it that you're going to go out with me—"

"I haven't said I would."

"Oh." He stopped jigging around. "Does that mean you won't?"

"I might," she said coyly. "If you ask me nicely . . ."

They spent that afternoon wandering around the town, drowning in a flood of words. Words bubbled out of them as if they'd known each other for years, and each knew immediately what the other was about to say. They talked incessantly, joyously, crazily; they talked like word machines. All the time they waved their hands about, emphasizing their words with gestures. To passers-by it must have seemed that never before had they seen such a close-knit pair.

"We could go camping," he said. "I know a spot."

"We could go horseriding."

"I've never had a horse. I had a rabbit once, but if you put a saddle on it, it just lay on the floor." He threw himself down to demonstrate.

"I don't care if everyone's laughing at us," Sadie cried. "I've never felt this way!"

"Neither have I," he said as he scrambled up again, and dusted off his palms on the waistband of his jeans. "You see that life line there?" he said, holding out his hand. "I'll live a thousand years."

"I'm sorry to disappoint you, but that's your heart line," she said. "It means you'll fall in love, and love for all of time. Your love will never fail. It will be the greatest love this world has ever known."

"Let me have a look at yours," he said.

"My line's broken," she said. "It's broken in three parts, which means three broken hearts. I'll have three desperate loves, each doomed to die, while you'll have just the one."

"That isn't *broken*," he said, "it's just wrinkled. See? It's the same as mine – almost identical."

"Maybe it's you," she said, and at once she stopped laughing.

11

The wind was howling through twisted tree tops, making the branches creak. Through blinding darkness she struggled up a hill, her hands slashed by the thorns which grew from tangled shrubs. The ground was so slick with dew that she pitched on her face, gulping in mud and dirt. But she could not slow down, for the pain was after her, bringing the fear and rage which lurk in maddened hearts. The pain was on the slope, chasing her like a beast. The pain was hunting her.

Tracey said, "What's it like taking your life in your hands every time you turn your back?"

"What?" Sadie stared blankly at her. "What are you talking about?"

"We heard you're seeing a lot of that fruitcake, Martin Kemp. It must be interesting dating a psychopath."

"I wouldn't know, Tracey."

"Does he show you his air gun?"

"Don't be ridiculous."

"Does he show you photos of the animals he's shot?"

"You're such a fool, Tracey." Sadie tried stepping past, but Tracey barred her way.

She said, "I took this photograph out of my father's files. Why don't you have a look? Everyone else has seen—"

Sadie snatched it out of her hands, and saw a small black cat with a hole between its eyes.

"Yes, very interesting," she said, handing it back. "Does your father know you're showing this stuff around school?"

"I just thought you ought to know," Tracey said, offering Sadie the kind of frozen smile which could put out a flame. "I thought you might be interested to know the kind of boy you're hanging out with now – A kitten-murderer."

"I'm not going out with him," said Sadie. "He's just a friend."

"Yes, well, with friends like that you don't need enemies."

"And I've always got you for that," Sadie said, pushing past and dropping one of her books. As she bent to pick it up Tracey kicked it away from her, and her group of cohorts laughed as Sadie snatched at it. Sometimes it was hard to know who was the worst person in her life, Tracey or Eleanor.

Sadie went to her English class and tried to force herself to pay attention. Tracey Scott wasn't really troubling her, because she had been through all that before; ever since they started school together Tracey had been a pain.

It was the new boy in her life, the laughing Tony Stern, who was occupying her thoughts. She couldn't stop thinking about him, no matter how she tried. Every time she closed her eyes she saw his smiling face. She found herself writing his name on her book covers, scribbling it constantly. It was like an obsession that was taking her over; more than a simple crush, less than a life-long love. She couldn't explain it herself, how he had so quickly become such an important part of her life.

But it was what she needed: somebody she could love, somebody of her own, with thoughts for her alone. Someone still untarnished by the evil ways and schemes of Tracey and Eleanor.

"Penny for your thoughts."

"Oh, not again, Martin!"

"The lesson's over," he said as he sat down on her desk. "Everyone's gone for lunch. There's only us two left."

Sadie looked round and gathered up her things. "I was miles away. Daydreaming idle thoughts."

Martin shifted his legs as she stood up to stuff her books away inside a bulging canvas bag. He'd tied a length of string around one of his thumbs, and it was cutting off the blood supply. He was beginning to worry because he'd knotted it so tightly that he couldn't undo it, and now it was swelling up. It had turned a shade of red he'd never seen before, and was throbbing alarmingly.

"I heard you fancy Maurice."

"Where did you hear that?" Sadie said, slipping her arm through the strap of the bag and heaving it off the desk.

"Maurice was saying it. He said he'd had the word that you were after him, wanting to go out with him."

"Maurice is dreaming," she said. "He's in the clouds. I wouldn't go with him if he was the last guy in the world. It was only my step-sister trying to stir things up, trying to make things hard for me."

"Oh," Martin grunted as he tried to lever off the string with his teeth and failed abysmally. "I'm not with him any more; we've kind of fallen out."

"That's good," Sadie replied. "You must have better friends than the stupid Cope brothers."

"Not really," Martin said. "There was only them

and you. I don't have other friends. You're the best one I've got. At least you talk to me."

Sadie said, "Lots of people will talk to you, Martin."

"No, they're all scared of me because I killed those cats." He looked her in the eyes. It was an intense look of pain and loneliness. "I'm always getting rejected by people, even my dad."

"Martin, your thumb's blue."

"I know," Martin replied. "I just wondered what it was like if you ever killed someone by tying a cord round them. It would be hard to strangle them, because they'd be fighting back." He looked down at the string, which was embedded in his thumb.

Sadie said, "Cut it loose. I think you've spent too long hanging around with Maurice Cope."

Sadie ran through black trees, towards the bleak, dark house which towered above the slope. It was a place of nightmares, or so the rumours told. A place haunted by ghosts and the cries of tortured souls. A place where dead men walked, and blood dripped from the walls on some nights of the year.

But it offered sanctuary from the monster on the slope; the monster which closed in with every desperate stride.

If she could only get to it. If she could only find the strength for one last mighty surge . . .

12

Maurice Cope's body was found under a hedge, with a rope tied round his neck. He had been knocked unconscious and strangled. The rope was a common sort, found in most hardware stores. The killer had used a length of wood as a fulcrum for the rope, as if applying a tourniquet.

This point was fairly interesting to the police who combed the scene, as it seemed to suggest the murder had been planned.

But it wasn't of much interest to the much-loathed Maurice Cope, who now had no thoughts at all . . .

"*Ow!*" Tony sucked his palm as he scrambled over a fence. "I've got a splinter."

He and Sadie were on the hillside overlooking the town, a steep incline of gorse, heather and stunted grass. It ascended from a stream which flooded in the spring, and gurgled like a child.

Some way below them lay the patchwork of their home; neat houses, towering spires, green meadows, rolling lawns. Still as a photograph, the only movement came from ripples on the Trent. The ripples were throwing sunlight back up towards the sky, turning the river into a long steel ribbon. The houses on the shores looked like boxes washed up in former, wilder times.

Ahead of them loomed the great, dark, brooding house of which Sadie had dreamed. Few people explored this site of death and doom seven decades before. It was a house where murder had stalked in the form of a mad old man consumed by jealousy.

Children occasionally played there, for a dare, but most people walked by, scarcely giving it a look. It was said that if you looked you might see the old man's face, and he would curse your name. Of course no one believed that, but they still hurried by, particularly on winter days when the old house creaked and groaned. Nobody looked inside to see where the groaning came from; they blamed it on the wind.

"The whole affair was caused by jealousy," Tony said. He was curious to look at the house and see what lay inside. Because he and Sadie were in love, they felt quite safe from harm. If they were ever going to look, this was the time to go, while their love ruled the world.

"Have you ever been inside?" asked Sadie.

"Never," he said, as he led her by the hand. "But I know a lot about it; I read it in a book. The man was Daniel Cross, and he married a teenage girl. She was thirty years younger than him and, for a time at least, they seemed quite happy together. But as he got older he started having dreams that she was cheating on him, going with a younger man, and he resolved to catch her out by hiding below stairs when she thought he'd gone into town.

"He waited all one day, in the cellar with the rats. He had an axe with him, and when it was dark he crept up the stairs and went to his wife's room. He found her with a young man, all right, and chopped him to pieces, but his wife ran out of the room and he chased her down the stairs. He chased her round the house while all the cooks and other staff tried to save her.

"In the end he caught and chopped her into bits; and he killed the others too, since they were witnesses. He dragged them all outside, and burned them on a fire that you could see for miles around."

The pair stopped for a breather and sat down on

the turf, gazing up at the house which dominated the scene. They could almost picture the blows of an axe cutting through bone, as black shutters banged in the breeze.

Tony tipped his head back to peer up at the sky. Long tracts of sullen cloud were spreading from the west, closing around the sun, sending chills through the air.

"And of course they caught him because they came to put out the fire, and he was dancing around, shouting demonic things. They say he was so mad that when they took him away he thought they were angels. He thought he was being rewarded for punishing evil, for stamping out the lust and depravity of the house. He thought he was a saint, acting on the word of God. He was quite bonkers."

"What did they do with him?" asked Sadie.

"Locked him up in the huge mental home that burned down in the war. They say that right to the end he was still walking around with a make-believe axe in his hands."

Sadie gave a shudder.

"Am I scaring you?" Tony said.

"Not too much. If he's dead – if there are no ghosts around."

"There are no ghosts," he said. "There's only you and me." He kissed her on the lips.

* * *

They padded up the steps of the dark, creaking house, and cowered in the porch.

"Do you want to go inside?"

"We've come this far," she said. She gave a nervous grin and clutched him by the hand.

He reached out to touch the door and a bird flew from the gloom, and they both let out a scream.

13

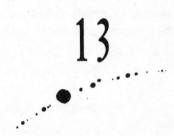

"Is this where it happened?" she asked.

"I suppose so," Tony said, as they stared down at the floor. They were in the hall, looking at a spot where a thin strip of wood had been gouged from the blackened boards as if hewn by an axe. It showed a ghostly pale against the dark brown stain which covered half the floor.

Sadie said, "That isn't blood, is it?"

"I don't think so; it's just damp."

"It still looks very fresh."

"Must be the atmosphere."

Tony stood up and wiped his hands clean. "He must have killed her here."

"This is a really creepy place," Sadie said, shuddering again.

"Do you want to look upstairs?"

"No thanks." She pulled a face. "Downstairs is quite enough."

Then a banging door put the wind up them, and they fled outside and tore off down the hill, laughing when nothing came after them.

They had reached the outskirts of town when Tony suddenly said, "Daniel Cross was my great-grandfather."

Sadie looked at him, astonished. "The man who killed them all?"

"Yes, he was my ancestor, the man who went insane, the wielder of the axe, the man who talked to God. That was my great-grandfather."

"I don't believe it!" Sadie said.

"Someone had to be," he said. "It's just unfortunate that it happened to be him. No riches in my past, no relatives of kings, just a crazy old man."

Sadie said, "But he killed them—"

"Not all of them," Tony said. "A baby got away. It was bundled up in some cloth. They think the maid did it when she saw what was going on. She hid it under some logs."

"And who was that, then?"

"That was my grandmother. She only died last year; her name was Mary Stern. She was christened Mary Cross, but she married a farm worker called Durkin Stern. He died years ago, at the beginning of the war. Got drowned during Dunkirk, or something weird like that. They never found his body. There's a lot of stuff like that in my family's past. I'm the only sane one!" He gave a little laugh. It was a nervous laugh, almost as if he felt ashamed.

He turned to look at Sadie.

"*I'm* not mad, you know," he said.

"I never thought you were," she said, taking his hand. She kissed him on the cheek. "It's all stuff from the past."

As the pair progressed through the town they found the way ahead blocked by a milling crowd. A line of police cars was parked beside a grass verge and a flashing ambulance stood with its back doors open wide. A stretcher in a field was covered with a cloth. A man was blubbering.

"*It is an omen!*" the man kept bellowing. "*It is a sign from God!*"

"Who's that?" Sadie whispered.

"Tommy Lane. He's another lunatic. He hangs around this part of town."

The pair moved closer, pushing slowly through the crowd. They could only get so far, then people refused to move. Sadie craned her neck to see, while Tommy Lane cried out again, "*This is an omen!*"

She spotted Martin, and grabbed him by the arm. "What's going on?" she asked.

"Maurice has been murdered. They'll probably think it was me because we had an argument in the High Street yesterday."

"Don't be stupid," said Sadie. "That's nothing new. Everyone argued with him – he was always looking for a fight."

"All the same, I'm pretty scared in case the police come round and want to question me."

"What have you got to worry about?" she asked, but she didn't hear whether Martin replied, because she was too busy trying to see. "Who's that man over there?" she asked.

"That's Maurice's dad," he said. "They found him in a bar." Then Martin pointed. "See that sign over there?"

Sadie squinted through the crowd at some words daubed on a wall in thick white paint.

"What does that mean?" she said. *"The Angel Walks Abroad."*

"I don't know," Martin said. "But the police took photographs. Maybe it's the Angel of Death—"

"More like a new rock band," Sadie said quietly.

14

Maurice's death sent out ripples which touched everyone. Parents became panic-stricken when their kids were late home from school. They drove them into town instead of letting them catch the bus. Melanie became quite paranoid about Sadie's boyfriend Tony.

"Why have we never met him? We don't know what he's like."

"What do you think he's like?" said Sadie. "He's a boy!"

"Well, yes, but what kind of boy? You've never brought him home."

"What for? For you to check?"

"Well, you have to be careful these days," said Melanie.

"Oh, sure; I'm walking round with a murderer on my arm. What do you think he's like? He's just a gentle boy—"

"He's Mary Stern's grandson."

"What's that got to do with anything?" said Sadie.

"She went mad, just like her father. She ended up in a home. The whole family's strange."

"Don't be ridiculous!" Sadie said angrily.

And then it started: another of their fights. They couldn't go for two days without a fight. In truth, it was Sadie who began most of them. Melanie just reacted.

"Why don't you mind your own business?" said Sadie.

"I'm only trying to help. It's because I'm concerned about you—"

"*Concerned!* Ha! That's a joke. You're always nosing into my private affairs." Sadie kicked off her shoes and strode out of the hall, slamming the kitchen door. Melanie went after her.

"You're always so secretive," she said as Sadie poured cold skimmed milk into a tall glass. "You never let us know where you're going or who you're with—"

"Why do you have to know?" Sadie glared at her stepmother ominously over the top of the glass. It left a thin white ring as she lowered it from her mouth and slammed it down on a marbled work surface, almost splintering it.

"It's nothing to do with you, you know, where I go or who I see. I'm not a little child or some kind of 'real' daughter. I'm just my *dad's* daughter, not yours – it's up to me to decide who I'll see."

"You're always so touchy." Melanie turned away. She put a hand to her hair, as if to check it was still there. She was a small woman, just on the point of changing from a size ten to a twelve. "I'm only trying to make a point."

Sadie snarled, "You've made your point. You're a nosey woman who wants to rule my life."

"Don't talk to me like that!"

"I'll talk to you how I like. You've got no hold on me."

In a flash of anger Sadie slammed the cutlery drawer with such ferocity that knives and forks jangled. So much bitterness was building up in her that she shocked herself.

Melanie looked at her, startled. "I was only asking," she said.

"But that's all you ever do; you keep right on asking things. I'm seventeen years old, and you've no right to interfere. I can look after myself."

Sadie picked her books up from the table by the door, glancing around the room as if she'd forgotten something. Even she could see that this wasn't the time to talk; she just felt too incensed.

She knew it wasn't Melanie's fault she was so upset; Melanie tried her best, and Sadie could see that. There were so many pressures on her life, and Maurice Cope's death was just the latest.

"Where are you off to now?"

"I'm going to my room." Sadie had to find some space before she said something she would really regret.

She lay down on her bed and stared up at the crack in the ceiling. It had been caused by her father stumbling around the loft when he was clearing up after they'd just moved house. They had been in the house less than a day when he slipped off a beam and almost brained himself. He had come down staggering, and everyone had laughed: Sadie, her mother and the friends who'd helped them move. He had tottered around the room giving a good impression of a man about to drop.

But they didn't seem to have days like that now; nobody laughed much. Life was too serious, too stressful, too intense. They needed more laughter – the kind of real laughter that Tony brought Sadie.

"Are you coming out tonight?" he said over the phone.

"I might," she murmured.

"What do you mean, you might?" he cried. "We haven't gone out for a week! You can't start standing me up!"

"I'm only teasing you."

"Oh, right." He seemed relieved. "Because I was going to tell you about this little kid today. He came into my dad's café, I guess with his mum and dad. And he was climbing on to a chair – he was only about three years old – and he, like, he *farted*. And it was a really loud one and everyone looked round, and his mum says – everyone was looking at them now – she says, 'What do you say, Simon?' And he has a big long think, and says 'Thanks very much!' Like he knew he had to say *some*thing, but he'd gone and got it wrong. He'd picked the wrong one out! Don't you think that's really great?"

"I think *you* are," she laughed. "You always make me smile."

"That's good," said Tony.

15

On her way to meet Tony, Sadie crossed the cobbled square in the centre of town. It was overlooked by shops holding up teetering roofs dating from Tudor times, and contained a fountain, seldom switched on now, because vandals kept filling it with washing-up liquid.

A narrow clock tower was the regular meeting place for the local pigeon flock, fed by kind "old dears". The pigeons had become so fat that they could barely move, and looked like cannonballs. They were cooing gently to each other about the day they'd had as Sadie caught her heel in a crack between the stones. She had to wrestle her shoe out, and as she stopped to slip it back on she heard somebody laugh.

They were over by the dry fountain, talking to a group of boys – the doubly dangerous team which had recently formed. There was her step-sister, Eleanor, and the latest friend she'd made, the cold-eyed Tracey Scott.

"Well, well, the Kiss of Death can't even cross the square without losing a shoe."

"Oh, push off, Tracey," Sadie said, still hopping as she wrestled on her shoe. "I hope your dress gets spoiled with all that pigeon muck."

"Ooh! Touchy, touchy!" Tracey started laughing and everyone else joined in, even though none of the boys quite understood why they were laughing so hard.

"She's got a boyfriend!" said Eleanor, smirking like a cat that's got the cream. "She's off to meet him now, aren't you, dear step-sister? Off to nibble his toes."

"What does he look like?" said Tracey.

"Like a frog. He's got sticking-out ears."

"He has not," Sadie said.

"And a big lump on his nose."

"Oh, push off, Eleanor; you haven't seen him yet."

Sadie kept on walking, but their laughter followed her right to the corner shop where Tony stood waiting. "What's everyone laughing at?" he said.

"Nothing." She took his arm. "Let's just get out of here."

*　　*　　*

They went to a small café which stayed open late at night and was a popular tourist trap. It had oak furniture which looked quite old, but was made by an ex-miner who lived on the outskirts of Nottingham. It took him half a day to age sixteen tables with ink and cold tea.

There they found a small corner booth and huddled over the menu, not wanting anything.

"I've missed you, Sade," he said.

"I've missed you, too," she said.

"It made my stomach hurt. I kept wondering what you were up to."

"I was probably thinking about you."

"Yes?" Tony grinned and his face lit up. He said, "Once every hour I tried to find a slot where I could say your name. I said it over and over, like some kind of ritual."

She said, "You're really mad."

"And I kept tossing a coin. I said, '*If it comes up heads, then she'll come out with me again. It it doesn't, she's gone off me.*'"

Sadie said, "What did it come up with?"

"It depends how long we're talking about. If we're talking the best of ten, then it was pretty close. But after about half an hour I think the 'ayes' had it by a slim majority."

"How many times did you toss it?"

"About a thousand and ten. There was nothing else I could do; I was only thinking of you. I think of you all the time. I can't get you out of my mind."

"That's how I feel about you."

It was such a relief to her to be with him – nobody in the world but the two of them; no one deriding her, no one heaping scorn on her. She could just be herself. She said, "I kept wondering why you've never been up there before."

"Where?"

"To that old house on the hill where your grandmother was born."

"I was kind of scared before. I never wanted to go near the place while I was all alone."

"But there must have been someone?"

"No one before you, Sade. I've never loved before; I'd never kissed a girl before."

"You're kissing me all right."

"That's because you're teaching me how to get it off pat."

A waiter watched them while they practised a little more, and he thought this wouldn't be his night for lifting massive tips. The way those two were going, it would be closing time before they came up for air.

That night Sadie dreamed about the old house.

She dreamed she was alone there, drifting from room to room. She dreamed she could hear ghosts howling under the stairs. She dreamed the banging doors were the footsteps of old Daniel, wandering around with his axe. He was looking for fresh victims to add to his roll of death, searching for someone else to take the place of his slaughtered wife.

Sadie looked at her hand and saw a wedding band gleaming against the skin.

"Hello."

"Martin?" she said. "It's very early in the day."

"I've brought you some flowers," he said.

Sadie stared at him with some embarrassment. "You shouldn't buy me flowers."

"It's okay, they were cheap." Martin held them out to her, and there was something almost forlorn about the way they drooped like half-dead snakes in his hands. "They're chrysanthemums," he said.

"I can see that," Sadie said.

"I bought them in town."

"It's very kind of you, but you shouldn't waste your money on buying flowers for me."

"It's not a waste," he said. "I really like you, and you're my only friend."

"Don't say that, Martin," she said. "You must have lots of friends."

"I haven't. Only you." He stood outside the porch like a cheap-rate undertaker. He was wearing an ill-fitting suit probably borrowed from his father's spare wardrobe. As potential suitors went,

Martin had a lot to learn about the ways of the world. "I know it's early, but I thought we might go for a walk."

"I don't think so," she said. "It's barely nine o'clock."

"Maybe we could sit outside?"

"Okay. If you like," she said. She led him round the back.

There was a well-kept lawn there and a red-brick patio. They sat on an old church bench which had been lovingly restored. Worshippers had sat there once, and now, like a strange echo, sat the adorer and the adored. For the embarrassed Sadie, this was the most bizarre moment she had faced for quite some time. Never in her wildest dreams could she have thought that when she got up today, Martin Kemp would come courting.

He said, "The police came round to see me yesterday, to talk about Maurice's death. They didn't think it was me who had done it, but they wanted to know what I thought. They wanted to know if I knew anyone who would be glad to see him dead. I couldn't be polite; I told them what I thought. I told them everyone."

Martin put the flowers down on the end of the varnished bench, easing them into the shade so they wouldn't wilt too much. It was too late for the flowers – he had bought them the previous night and had since failed to water them.

"It seems kind of funny," he mused, "because they said they'd heard the same. Maurice didn't have any friends, he just had enemies. The only one who seemed to care was his younger brother, Steve. Even his dad seemed quite pleased."

"Martin – why are you telling me this?"

"I'm not sure," he murmured. "I just wanted you to know that the murderer wasn't me."

"I never thought it was."

"Some people thought it was. I think Steve thought it was." Martin put his hand down to move the flowers a touch. His dark hair slid over his eyes, and he had to flick it back. He looked awkward and stiff in a suit which was far too warm for this increasingly humid day.

He wasn't the only one who felt that way; Sadie felt a little stiff herself. She didn't know what to say to him, or what he was doing there. She didn't know whether he'd come to ask her out, or to get things off his chest. She didn't want to encourage him.

In fact the only thing she could think about was the fact that, at this time, they had something in common that few others would have. Among all their friends, they were probably the only ones receiving therapy. Martin's was common knowledge, while Sadie's own treatment was known only to a few. And because it was so secret she had a desire to know much more about it.

Was she going crazy or was she just one of many who went through the same? Did everyone else have the same doubts as her, or did they handle things without difficulty?

So without actually telling Martin that she had been there herself, she began to steer their conversation towards therapy, until finally she asked him straight out, hoping he wouldn't mind, hoping he would understand.

"What does the doctor say," she asked, "when you go for therapy?"

"What?" Martin had been miles away. He dragged his thoughts back. "Do you mean when I go to the hospital?"

Sadie nodded. "What's it like? What does she say to you?"

"It's a him," Martin murmured. "And he doesn't say too much. It's a quiet half hour. We mostly sit there staring, like we don't know what to say, and every now and then he asks me about something. What kind of sports do I like? What kind of games do I play? Mostly small talk like that."

Sadie said, "Does he ever ask you about your air gun?"

"Do you mean when I killed the cats?" Martin seemed quite at ease discussing all this stuff. Maybe he realized that he would never get very far if he kept things bottled up.

He undid his shoelaces – his feet were killing

him. He loosened his blue silk tie and pulled it down a shade. He wiped his sweating hands on the sides of his grey trousers, and said, "Sometimes he does. Not all the time, though; we don't talk about it every week. Mostly it's things like, *Do I dream? Who are the people that I love?*"

"Who *do* you love?" she asked.

"I love my mum and dad and, oddly enough, those cats," he murmured quietly. "That's why I can't understand why I did it – I really liked those cats. I used to play with them, with paper balls and things. That's the really scary part – that I still can't understand why I had to kill them all."

His gaze slid away from her, across the lawn, as if the answer lurked somewhere among the trees. He said, "My mother didn't – she kept chasing them off. She was always putting nuts out, and the cats hunted the birds. And they messed in our garden instead of messing in their own. One day I saw my mum go out and throw some stones to try to chase them off.

"I thought maybe I could help her, so I took my brother's gun and sat up half the night, and shot them when they came. It wasn't that easy, although I'd put food down, because it was pitch black outside. I had to keep dazzling them with a torch, then shooting them. And the hardest part was that they kept coming out, as if they wanted it.

"Even the last one – you'd think it would have

been scared to death but it still wandered in, just waiting to be shot. It was almost as if the cats all knew that they'd done something wrong and had to be punished for it. They kept on coming, and I kept shooting them. Even when they were dead, I kept on shooting them." Martin's eyes looked blank as they stared through the trees, seeing nothing at all.

Sadie said, "What does your psychiatrist say?"

"Nothing. He just listens."

She said, "Does it bother you?"

"Seeing a psychiatrist?" After some thought he gave a shrug, and reached down to his shoes to tie the laces up. "Not as much as killing those cats did. I really liked those cats. I'm sometimes terrified I might kill something else." As if he felt he'd said too much, he rose to his feet, and said, "This was a bad idea. I know that you don't mind me, but you don't want to go out with me." He gave her a half-sad smile as he eased his jacket off, slung it across his back and pushed his thick hair back. "It doesn't matter though."

Sadie rose beside him and pecked him on the cheek. She said, "It was nice of you to bring me the flowers, Martin."

He looked down ruefully, saying, "But I let them die. I should have watered them."

16

The next day Stephen Cope was found lying behind some bins, as dead as his brother. He had been clubbed to death, and then shot several times with a high-powered air-rifle. It was a need-less act, whose only purpose seemed to be dis-figurement. Maybe it was because he kept staring, even after he was dead, and the killer couldn't face that last accusing stare, or maybe it was sheer rage on the killer's part.

Whatever the motive, it was a particularly nasty crime, and the policemen at the scene frequently looked away from the body. They didn't want to gaze on the killer's work more than was necessary.

"Sadie?"

"*Ooh!*" Sadie shrieked as Martin's face appeared

at the bottom of the garden. "You frightened the life out of me!"

"I'm sorry," he whispered. His face was tense and flushed, his eyes were glancing round. He said, "I came across the fields – I kept on tripping up. The police are after me."

Sadie stared past him.

"Not *right* behind," he said. "But they'll think it was me, trying to protect myself. Stephen told a lot of people that he thought I killed Maurice, and that I was going to have to pay. You have to help me – I have to get away."

"Where are you going to go?"

"I have to hide somewhere."

"Don't be ridiculous, Martin. This isn't a Hollywood film; you have to face the police."

"What if they blame me?"

"They won't blame you," she said.

"I didn't kill him, Sade—"

"Then go and tell the police."

"But they'll think I used the same air gun that I used to shoot the cats. They'll think I brought it out. It's been locked away for months now, somewhere at the back of the loft—"

"Then show the police where it is. They can do tests on it."

"I'm scared." Martin gripped the fence. He looked like a hunted beast, not the Martin of yesterday. "What if they frame me?"

"Why should they want to do that?"

"I don't know," Martin said. "But you read about these things. I go to a psychiatrist – I've used a gun myself—"

"Martin, I'll come with you."

This touch of sanity seemed to calm Martin down, and he said, "No, it's okay, I'll go with my mum and dad. They'll tell me what to say. Maybe I walked in my sleep. Maybe I did kill him."

"Don't talk like that!"

"I'm getting so confused." Martin glanced round again, his eyes scanning the fields. He almost seemed to think that some kind of lynch mob would burst upon the scene. "I fought with both of the Copes – they're both people I knew."

"Martin, we *all* knew them. You've got nothing to worry about."

"That's easy for you to say because no one will think it was you, but they're all going to look at me. I feel like I'm being set up, and someone's after me."

"You're being paranoid."

"But that's how it seems to me." Martin rubbed at his face, spreading dirt from his hands to his hot, sweating cheeks. "Someone's using me, trying to set me up. I've really had it, Sade."

Sadie tried her best to say something that would make things seem okay, but the sight of Martin's eyes froze the words in her throat. He looked so sad and scared, so lost and all alone. He looked like a frightened child.

17

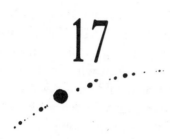

Sadie stood outside the old house, gazing up at the blank, uncurtained windows. She wasn't sure why she had come there, other than that the recent deaths had made her think morbid thoughts, and she had been drawn to look at the house of death.

This was a place of slaughter and terrible revenge, a place where jealous rage had almost killed a line. Only one child had remained, and from that fragile link the blood-line carried on to her boyfriend. How precious was this line, and how frail its grip on life! If Sadie herself died then her whole line would cease, snuffed out without a trace.

She was not morbid by nature, but Death's gaze is something which all of us must face – a blank visage which can, at times, hypnotize us all.

Thus it was with Sadie as she crept into the house. Death's hand beckoned her on, inviting her to look. Death's voice said, *"See the place where my works were performed. Come, see my mansion . . ."*

She pushed back the heavy door, and stood inside the hall gazing up at the stairs. Still she was uncertain of what she was looking for: perhaps some hint, some sign, some clue of why Death rears his head. Something which would let her know whether she would be the next, or whether she'd be safe.

She crept up the creaking stairs, holding a banister rail smooth as an apple. The air was musty; dust swirled inside thin shafts of pale orange sunlight that filtered from above. The dust could be the dust that the dead themselves had breathed so many years before.

She looked into the bedrooms, and saw the very bed in which mad Daniel Cross had confronted his young wife. His pillow was still there, with a hollow where his head lay dreaming poisoned thoughts.

Moving on slowly she passed through every room, seeing clear signs of change, such as litter on the floor. Vagrants had sometimes used the house as shelter from the storms which could sweep down from the moors. They had left graffiti crudely scrawled on the walls. *Old Daniel got quite "Cross" and choppered off her head . . .* They had left an old blanket and a broken thermos flask; they had left their empty cans.

But what most surprised Sadie was how little *had* been changed; how much of the original furniture and trappings still remained, as if all those who'd come had been afraid to disturb the dust of time strewn over them. There was an almost shrine-like feel about the house; a sense of wary peace, of torments laid to rest. A sense that death, once loud, was just a whisper now, an echo in the walls.

Moving on, Sadie tried to relate all of this to her new love Tony Stern. It seemed impossible that he could have been linked to this, for he was the precise opposite of his mad great-grandfather, so gentle and full of life, so tender and caring. They must have different blood. She couldn't imagine him possessed of such a rage as would wipe out four souls in a fit of jealous pique. If he bore his ancestor's genes he had successfully distilled them with his own.

Maybe that was why he had never visited the house before; he must feel so removed from the madness of the past. Only with her at his side did he find the strength to face his family's history.

So it was somewhat puzzling to her to find her boyfriend's name scratched on the kitchen wall, as if by the point of a knife. It was in the centre of a heart, and there was another name below it. The name was *Tracey Scott*.

18

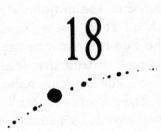

"**D**o you know Tracey Scott?" she asked as Tony took her hand and led her through the park.

Tony seemed a little surprised by this, and murmured, "Tracey Scott? Yes, I knew her for a while."

"Did you go out with her?"

"I might have done," he said.

"What do you mean, you might have done?"

He looked a little awkward. "Well, yes, I went out with her," he said, not facing her. "But it all happened a long time ago, and we never went out for long."

"But you took her to that house."

"Which house?"

"The 'family' house, that you said you'd never seen."

He said, "Is this an inquisition, Sade?" trying to keep things light, trying to cool the rage he could see growing in her. "We went there once or twice, that's all – it didn't count. It meant something with you."

"How long did you go out with her?"

"I don't know . . . seven weeks." Tony shrugged, as if this meant nothing. He was staring through the park, as if to find something that would distract them both. "It was just a brief thing, and it never got anywhere. Tracey wasn't my type, and I wasn't really hers. We had a few dates and then we rowed a lot, and I broke it off with her."

"Why didn't you tell me?"

"Why do you think?" Tony replied. "You two don't hit it off, so I said nothing. It wouldn't have helped things much to say that she and I had had a thing going."

Sadie gave a brief snort. "Why did you break it off?"

"I just said – it didn't work; we never hit it off."

"You must have liked her, though."

"I did at first. It didn't last for long." Tony looked uncomfortable. "It's like you and Dave," he went on. "You never talk about him."

Sadie said, "That's different, because he's not around."

"He's back in town," Tony said. "He's working at the bank."

"What?" Sadie felt numb. "David's back in town?"

"He's been back a couple of weeks."

"I didn't know," Sadie said at last.

"I thought you would have heard," Tony muttered quietly. He turned to look at her. "You're not the only one who gets jealous, you know. We all feel that way sometimes."

"Why didn't you say something?"

"What? That your boyfriend's back? Sounds like the title of a song." He walked away from her and sat down on a bench, his hands hanging loosely between his thighs. He scraped a patch of dirt with the heel of his left shoe, and glanced around the park.

"I didn't really want to come running round shouting 'Your boyfriend's back!' He's not the Number One spot on my talking charts. I'd rather he'd stayed away, if I'm going to be honest about it."

"How did he look?" she asked.

"Oh, he looked flipping marvellous!" said Tony bitterly. "Why don't we ask him out? We can all go for a meal."

"That's not what I meant," she said.

"What *did* you mean?" he asked.

"I'm not sure," she mumbled. It took a bit of

adjusting to, knowing that Dave was back. She didn't know whether it was good or bad, whether to smile or to be sad. She didn't want him to interfere with her friendship with Tony, but she felt curious.

What did he look like after those months away? How would he feel about her if they should chance to meet? He had often sworn that he would look after her, and take good care of her. He had always been jealous, and couldn't stand to see a boy so much as look at Sadie in the street. How was he going to feel now she had someone else? Would it bother him at all?

"Does he know you're going out with me?" she asked.

Tony gave a shrug. "I didn't go rushing up to tell him all our news."

"He used to be a very jealous sort."

"It seems we're all that way," Tony said quietly. "We've all got our little secrets – the little things we've done that we don't talk about."

"I was always honest with you," she said. "I've never lied to you."

Tony gave a deep sigh. "Not like I lied?" he said. He glanced up at her. "I really like you, Sade."

"I like you too," she said, giving him a smile which didn't seem quite real.

The sudden reappearance of her former boyfriend

caused confusion in Sadie's mind. Would it pose a threat to Tony's trust in her? How would he handle it?

If he acted sensibly, then nothing would go wrong. If it made him too upset, then trouble was in store. Sadie had seen real jealousy in her time with Dave, and it wasn't a pretty thing.

Jealousy is vicious, and lashes out like a snake. It hurts the one it loves, and won't play second best. There could be tricky times ahead if Dave turned his attentions to Sadie again.

It was just one more problem on top of those she already had. Tracey and Eleanor, the desperate Martin Kemp and now the jealousy of love. As for the Copes, Sadie knew it wasn't just Martin Kemp who had gained by their death: she too had felt a great weight lift from her back.

In a strange way, she felt that maybe someone out there was looking after her.

How far would they go, to keep her safe from harm? What if they made a mistake and chose the wrong target?

Sometimes she found herself wondering how many people knew just how afraid she'd been of Maurice and Stephen Cope. Would her unseen protector help her if she got into more trouble? Would they always keep her safe?

19

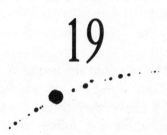

The next night someone threw a brick through Sadie's bedroom window.

It landed on the dressing table, smashing a small mirror and knocking her perfume to the floor. The bottle didn't break until she jumped out of bed and slammed her foot on it.

Sadie screamed as the glass gouged through her foot and pain shot up her leg. Her father burst into the room and tumbled over her in a moment of mayhem.

"What's going on?" he yelled.

"I've cut my foot open! There's broken glass everywhere! I'm bleeding all over the rug!"

"Don't panic, Sade!" he cried. "Where's the light-switch? What's that smell?"

"It's perfume!" Sadie howled. "It's not even the good stuff—" She crashed down on the bed and blood splattered on the wall as she waved her foot around. "It hurts! It hurts!" she cried.

Her father stumbled over something and said, *This is a brick!*

"I know!" she yelled at him. "Somebody threw it in!"

"What? Threw it into the room?"

"No, they threw it at the cat and the cat brought it in here! Of course they threw it into the room! Why do you think I'm rolling around with this glass in me?"

Maybe it was the unfortunate timing (it was just after 3.00 a.m.), but everything Sadie said seemed to make matters more confused. It took her father several minutes to understand what had happened. By that time Sadie was almost fainting from the pain which lanced through her foot, and a shell-shocked Melanie had to take her to Casualty for stitches while her father rushed outside, flailing his cricket bat and waving his torch around.

20

"So what's it all about?" Melanie said quietly. "Tell me what's going on."

Sadie looked at her, startled. "Don't ask me," she muttered. "I didn't throw the thing – go and ask whoever did."

"It's not just the brick," Melanie said. "I think that's just a part of what you're doing these days. It's the people you're hanging around with, the company you keep." She jammed the car keys home and pulled her seat-belt tight. "That boyfriend of yours, and the fact that you seem ashamed to invite him round to the house."

"Don't be so ridiculous – I'm not ashamed of him!"

"Then don't keep sneaking round with him

behind our backs." Melanie slammed the car into gear, and eased it from its slot outside the hospital.

They headed home through the light of dawn, which hung like a grey mist over the deserted streets. They startled prowling cats, who thought they owned the world at that hour of the day.

As the blue car rolled onwards, low hills came into view, hills grey as fresh-cut slate, old as time itself. They were shrouded by thin cloud which foretold rain.

Sadie looked across the car. "I don't sneak around with him."

"You know what I'm talking about," Melanie said, changing gear. "I've seen you in the hills, creeping round that old house like you're scared to be seen. If this boy's everything you say he is, don't be ashamed of him."

"I'm not ashamed of him!" Sadie said, half amazed.

"Then bring him to the house."

"What for? For you to grill? For Eleanor to goad?"

Sadie thought Melanie must be dreaming if she thought she'd fall for that. She would not bring Tony home for Eleanor to mock.

Melanie steered around a curve, then pulled into the side of the road and eased the handbrake on. She twisted sideways. "I'm not going to grill you, Sade, and I'm not going to grill your friend; that's not what I'm talking about. It's just that in times like these, with a killer on the loose, you can't be too careful. And that old house is creepy – it's got a bad history."

"I know all about the house."

"Do you know there were murders there?"

Sadie stared at the road.

"And do you know what happened after that?"

"Yes." Sadie gnawed on a thumbnail.

Melanie killed the engine and ran a hand through her hair. She looked tired, as though this was all quite a strain. Maybe it was; Sadie didn't help much when it came to bridge-building.

"Did you know that Tony's grandmother spent her life in a mental home?"

"What does that have to do with him? It's not hereditary."

"No," Melanie agreed. "But you ought to know this: there's been trouble all along. His young mother killed herself, and a sister died. That entire family seems cursed by poisoned blood."

Sadie snorted. "There's no such thing," she said.

"No, I don't suppose there is. You ought to take care, though; you ought to watch yourself."

Melanie started the car again and eased it from the kerb.

"We've got enough problems without fretting over you. It's not fair on your dad."

"Don't drag him into this."

"He frets the most of all."

The car leapt forward to beat a changing light, and almost killed a bird which bolted from a hedge. They both thought they caught a glimpse of the wanderer, Tommy Lane, asleep in undergrowth.

"Everyone you know now seems to be odd in some way: that strange boy Martin Kemp, and the brothers who got killed. And now this Tony Stern – and Eleanor tells me David's back in town."

"I might have known she'd come into it," Sadie said sullenly. "Does she fancy Dave herself?"

"Don't be ridiculous. It's you I'm worried about; it's you I'm talking about. What are you up to? What are you trying to prove?"

"I'm not trying to prove anything," Sadie said, giving a shrug.

"If you could learn to trust us more . . ."

Melanie let it drop. It seemed a waste of time.

As the car braked on the gravel drive Sadie opened the door and swung her sore foot out. Her wounds had been cleaned up and stitches put in place, but a pain like throbbing heat was pulsing through her leg. It would be agony to walk for the next few days and she'd have to sleep with her foot propped up.

But as she slammed the car door, she found herself pondering on the fact that without Melanie's help that trip could have been much worse. No one likes hospitals, but Melanie had done her best to take her mind off it.

Maybe her step-mother wasn't too bad, given half a chance. If she could just cut down on the constant lecturing . . .

Sadie stared across the car. "Thanks, Melanie," she said.

"You're welcome," Melanie replied.

21

"Well well! So the stupid Kiss of Death has slashed her own foot to get some attention."

"Oh, push off, Eleanor."

"No, let me guess, Sade," Eleanor said as she dragged a chair across the rug. "This was a suicide attempt, but you managed to miss your wrist because your fingers slipped."

"It wasn't funny," Sadie said wearily.

"No, but it made *me* laugh," Eleanor said as she straddled the seat. "I bet you made a fuss. I bet you howled and screamed."

"Sometimes you're such a child." Sadie put her book down. It was pointless trying to read; she would get no rest at all while Eleanor was around.

She said, "How come you're not with your big mate then, that 'angel' Tracey Scott?"

Eleanor gave a shrug. "She's doing something else. Maybe she's making plans to take your boy-friend back, that love-struck Romeo."

Sadie said, "He never liked her."

"That's what you think," Eleanor said. "While she was going out with him he would never leave her alone. That's why she called it off, because she couldn't take his jealousy."

"That's utter rubbish."

"Is it?" Eleanor gave a smile. "She could have Tony back with one wave of her hand. You should have seen the stuff he wrote to her! Really pathetic stuff. He swore he loved her and he'd never let her go. He said he would kill anyone who tried to get in his way. He was really mad for her; he nearly killed himself when she stopped going with him."

"So why is he going out with me, then?" Sadie said scornfully.

"Trying to make Tracey mad, I suppose; make her jealous. Who knows?" Eleanor shrugged, reaching round to a bowl and grabbing a ripe peach. She took a juicy bite, and said over her hand, "He's an utter psychopath. He's worse than Martin—"

"Don't be ridiculous."

"He's the biggest creep of all. He always carries a knife. He said he'd cut her heart out if she cheated on him. That's why she finished with him."

"I don't believe you!" Sadie said angrily.

Eleanor shrugged again. "Suit yourself," she said carelessly. She took a second bite, and juice ran down her hand. She shook it at the floor.

Sadie stared at her helplessly. *Why is she doing this? Why does she have to spoil the only thing I have?* Sadie had looked inside Tony's heart and seen the goodness there – he was no psychopath.

Surely such people stood out so that you could see it in their eyes? Surely all dangerous madmen walked with a clear, distinctive walk? Surely – but did they? Wouldn't they look as normal as anybody else? If they gave out clues, they'd soon be caught. The biggest of them all must have looked like any boy who ever went to school.

But she trusted Tony, despite these fears and doubts; trusted him with the love she had given him. Wasn't this just Eleanor, provoked by jealousy, trying to stir things up? Surely that must be the answer – it was just jealous spite, nothing but Eleanor's hatred. Who did she trust more, Eleanor or Tony Stern? Whose words did she believe?

"Are you listening to me?" Eleanor said.

"What?" Sadie glanced up. Her eyes were as dark as night, and filled with bitter rage.

Her poisonous stepsister was trying to ruin her life. Some day she would have to pay.

22

"Sadie!"

"What?" Sadie turned around painfully as Martin Kemp put on a spurt to catch her up. The market square was crowded, and he had to weave his way through hordes of boys on bikes and mothers pushing prams, dodging a man heaving a washing machine on to the back of a van.

As he caught up with her he said, "Remember that sign? The one that was written on the wall near where Maurice was murdered? It said *'The Angel walks'.* Well, take a look at this." He showed Sadie a page from last night's newspaper.

He had ringed the spot in pencil, and it stood out like a torch between two lonely-hearts.

"What do you think?" said Martin.

"I don't know," Sadie replied.

"Do you think it means something?"

Sadie shook her head.

The message said *"The Angel walks abroad, and if you listen hard you'll hear her beating wings . . ."*

23

Sadie showed the newspaper ad to her psychiatrist at their next meeting.

Mrs Cox read it carefully, then took her glasses off. She put them on her desk, and adjusted them a touch. "Why do you think this relates to you?" she said.

"Just the wings," Sadie said. "I see wings in my dreams."

"This message could be meant for anyone," Mrs Cox said quietly. "Do you feel some special bond with this ad? Is there something beyond the words – some secret meaning there which no one else can see?"

Sadie was silent, thinking. There *was* a message there, though she couldn't say quite what. And yes, it struck a chord; it echoed in her heart like the coming of a storm. She had once had a golden labrador. The dog was frightened of noise, and could hear storms coming. Long before thunder appeared the dog would disappear, to hide under a bed.

She said, "There's something, but I can't say what it is – a link between the words and my problems. The phrase 'The Angel of Death' is very like what people sometimes call me. They call me the *Kiss* of Death."

Mrs Cox said, "But it doesn't say that much. It says, *The Angel walks . . .*"

"But the meaning's pretty clear. The phrase was there when Maurice Cope died and now it's here again, warning of other deaths."

Mrs Cox poured some iced water into a crystal glass. She offered it to Sadie, who refused, then sipped it herself. The ice tinkled like jewels as she put the tumbler down and wiped away a lipstick smudge. "Maybe you're reading too much into this – these ads are often strange. People make them 'mysterious' to get people to look."

"But I think . . ." Sadie frowned deeply. "You asked me if I felt some special bond with this. Well, the truth is, I *do* feel that this was meant for me. I don't know why that is, other than that it strikes a chord. I think someone out there knows the things I dream about and is almost *goading* me."

"And who would know about them, other than you and I?"

Sadie shrugged. "Maybe my step-sister, if she's looked at my book. And she might tell all her friends, particularly Tracey Scott, who *is* an 'angel'."

"What do you mean, 'an angel'?"

"That's what she calls herself. If anything bad happens, she says it wasn't her. She says, 'It couldn't be me, because I'm far too nice. I'm an angel.'"

"I take it you don't like her?" Mrs Cox said after a pause.

"Not much." Sadie looked down and fiddled with her thumbs. "She's always taunting me, and now it seems that I've got her old boyfriend." She looked up suddenly. "Do you think that's enough to make her *mad* enough to want to harm me?"

"What do you think?"

"I don't know," Sadie said, looking down at her locked thumbs again. "It doesn't seem very likely that she would kill people, even if the Cope brothers were a particular pain to her. They were always after her, mocking her, for not going out with them." She glanced upwards. "She's very popular. Most of the boys in town seem to have dated her. The only ones who didn't were David and the Cope brothers. They never liked her that much."

"She *must* be popular," the psychiatrist said wryly.

"Yes." Sadie gave a smile. "All the boys love Tracey. It kind of makes you sick, but then I've got Tony, so what should I worry for?"

Mrs Cox said, "This advert – I think it's just a joke. It wasn't meant for you, but you've latched on to it. It's probably two people having an illicit love affair."

"You're probably right," said Sadie.

"You've been much better lately, so don't start tensing up because of someone else. Let them do what they want; don't start getting confused by other people's dreams." Mrs Cox picked the glass up and took another drink. She said, "The world is huge, and it's not all aimed at you."

"I'm getting paranoid."

"You're reading too much into other people's words."

After that the pair talked idly about more general things: the hot weather, the increasing swarms of wasps. They touched on Sadie's dreams only fleetingly. They were diminishing now.

24

Over the next few days, more messages appeared in the press. They were always about the same thing: the "beating of the wings". They all referred to angels or revenge, and talked of pain and death, and hunting through the town for the next victim. Most people thought they were very sick jokes, but Sadie disagreed. She truly believed they were put there to spread fear. She thought the town's killer was warning in advance that he would strike again.

What seemed most perplexing was that the ads had not been banned, and that the local police appeared singularly unmoved. Sadie thought they should have moved in to trace the source of the ads, and pick the killer up.

But maybe it was more complicated than that; maybe the police had tried to act. Maybe they allowed the ads through to tease the killer out. Maybe they knew his name, but couldn't yet find the proof to lock someone away.

Whatever the reason the ads kept showing up, and Sadie cut them out and stuck them in her book. She thought they showed how to draw the killer out, if one could but read the signs.

The cordless telephone rang while she was alone inside the house, examining the ads. She picked it up carelessly, and said, "Hello, who's this?"

A voice said, "Sade, it's me . . ." and the breath froze in her throat. It went on, "How are you?"

"I'm okay," Sadie whispered. She could find nothing more to say. It was a shock to hear David's voice again and she felt her senses swim. They had never said goodbye, and somehow because of that things weren't quite over yet. Yet at the same time she was free of him, because she had Tony. As she reached round for a stool she felt like a mountain goat, teetering on a rocky ledge.

David said, "I've been waiting, trying to find the guts to phone. I've still not found them, but this could have gone on for years. I thought I ought to phone just to see how you are."

"I'm fine," she said again.

He said, "It didn't work out, being on that

college course. I never liked the place, and I kept thinking of you."

"I suppose that's why you never wrote."

He said, "I kept trying to, but I didn't know what to say. I felt so lonely—"

"You could have said something."

"It seemed so pitiful to keep bleating on all the time. I wanted to say something that would make you feel happy, not disappointed with me."

"Why should I be disappointed?" Sadie pushed her long hair away from the phone. She put a thumb to her lips, and idly chewed the nail, staring at a dark spot on the wall where paint had splashed when her dad last did the doors.

"Because I went away to try to *be* something, and couldn't handle it."

"There's nothing wrong with that."

"I thought I'd let you down. I thought I'd look a fool in front of all our friends."

Sadie pulled her thumb from her mouth, and frowned down at the nail. "You should have said something if you were struggling."

"I know. I've lost it all, wasted everything. I lost the course and you."

She didn't offer him any sympathy, because it wasn't due. Nor did she hang up the phone – she was too confused. She just stayed on the line, listening to David breathe, wondering how he looked now.

After a time he asked her, "Could we go out again?"

"I don't think so," she said. "I've got a new boyfriend now."

"But could we meet sometime?"

"What for? What would be the point?"

David couldn't answer her.

25

She met him anyway, just to see how he looked now; just to see if she felt the same about him. Dark-haired and handsome, he still had the power to melt her heart, but Sadie was aware of a distance between them which had never been there before. Though he might soften her heart, he wouldn't be able to twist her around his little finger again.

They met in a coffee shop which they had often used before. A place where lovers sat in small, dark booths. But they weren't lovers now; they had been too long apart and other things had intervened.

"So – how are you keeping?" he asked.

Sadie shrugged. "I'm not too bad. Melanie's with us now, so of course that means Eleanor."

"Your favourite human being."

"My favourite hunting dog. She's always after me." Sadie picked up a spoon, and swirled it in her mug. The thick, creamy head on her coffee disappeared. "Lots of strange things are going wrong. Did you hear about the Cope brothers?"

Her old boyfriend nodded. "No one seemed too upset. I would have killed them myself if they'd ever bothered you."

"They always bothered me. They bothered everyone." Sadie blew on her coffee. "And you're so ridiculous – all this talk of killing people. One of the worst things you ever did was say that you'd kill someone. Your jealousy's a pain – did I ever tell you that?"

"All the time," he murmured. But he was smiling as he reached to take her hand.

She pulled it away and said, "Don't start that now. It's over between us; you can't mess people around and just expect to walk back."

"What do I have to do, then?"

She stared away from him, gazing through the leaded panes on to a quiet street. She said, "Don't do anything. I don't want you back. This is for old time's sake."

"You mean you don't like me?"

"I don't want to go out with you." She lifted up her mug and sipped the hot coffee. "I'll see you as a friend, but that's as far as it goes."

"That's not enough for me." David leaned

forward. "I really want you, Sade. I'd do anything to have you back again. I always did my best to keep you safe from harm."

"Do you think that's love?" Her eyes flicked upwards, to gaze into his own. Once she would have been lost in their sensual depths, but now they just looked like any other eyes, their magic long gone. She said, "It isn't enough, you know, to be insanely jealous. It's a restrictive thing that binds people with chains."

"I just wanted to make you mine, keep you safe from the things that threatened to harm you."

"What kind of things?" she asked, somewhat exasperated.

"Well – people like the Copes, who kept on hanging round you. It wasn't jealousy, it was protectiveness."

"They seemed much the same."

She turned away again, and stared out on the street, where a blond-haired boy was pedalling a bike and mothers were parading babies in prams. "Anyway, it's over now."

David took a deep breath. "I'll still watch out for you."

Sadie kept on looking out, and the boy fell off his bike. She could hear his wailing cries, see the mothers rush to help.

"Do what you like," she sighed.

*   *   *

When she got back to the house it seemed un-usually quiet, although the car was parked outside. Her father must have come home early – perhaps he was out the back. She could hear nothing in the stillness of the rooms, but she could sense some-thing upstairs; maybe a shadow moved, maybe a breath eased out.

She had started to climb the stairs when her father's face appeared, ashen and leaded-eyed, looking down at her. He said, "We're both up here."

She kept on climbing, and said, "What's going on?" There was something chilling about the way her father stood. It was as if he had lost his bones, and it was only strength of will which kept him standing up.

He said, "A phone call. We've got to go into town."

"What for?"

"The hospital – something's happened to Eleanor."

"What kind of thing?" she asked.

"She's dead. The police phoned up. Somebody murdered her . "

26

She had been found on the edge of town with deep knife wounds in her chest, and a scarf wrapped round her neck. The scarf was Sadie's: Eleanor had borrowed it. Sadie wasn't going to want it back now.

Sadie sat alone and scared in her quiet bedroom, while Melanie sobbed downstairs. She was trying not to think about the horror of the death, which had been painful and slow. Her step-sister had bled to death while somebody stood and watched, making sure she didn't get up.

Sadie kept on shaking as her mind pictured the scene: the pain on Eleanor's face, the killer's gloating eyes. They must have stood so close that they might have exchanged a kiss, but the knife-blade intervened.

How did it seem to Eleanor, knowing she was about to die? Knowing that that great pain was the last she'd ever feel? Knowing that she would breathe no more, and that the air inside her lungs was the last she would ever taste?

The whole scene was so terrible that Sadie tried to shut it out, but the harder she tried, the clearer the vision became.

The knife-blade through the heart. The two bodies so close. The last despairing look . . .

27

The days drifted by until the funeral. It took place on a Friday. The sky was clear, the sun beating down as if to scorch the ground. Insects patrolled the lawns, and their soft buzzing sounds were the only noises heard. The house seemed so empty that it felt unnatural, and as Sadie stood in Eleanor's room she could have been the last thing on earth. In the silence she could sense so many tiny details which had escaped her before.

She could smell Eleanor's perfume still hanging on the air, and almost feel her breath drifting across the room. The chairs seemed so empty, and even posters on the walls seemed somehow lonely. It was these small things which emphasized the loss: the half-used box of talc, the lipstick on a towel, the clothes still strewn around waiting to be picked up.

Where were all these things going to go? Who was going to pick them up? Who was going to sort them out and pack them into boxes? Who was going to find the strength to say, "This is the end, and Eleanor must leave"?

Or would they stay there for ever as mementoes of the past, like the teddy-bear on a chair, which had clung on through the years? Would he cling on some more, decaying, gathering dust, slowly falling apart?

Sadie turned round at a soft sound to see her father, his grey suit neatly pressed, a parting in his hair. He was trying to fix his tie, which stubbornly refused to lie straight on the shirt.

His grey eyes watched her. "This will be very hard," he said.

"I know," she said softly, as she helped him fix the tie.

"There will be lots of people there who won't know what to do, or how they should react. So they'll stand around awkwardly, saying all the wrong things, because there are no things to say at times like this."

"I know." She had been there before. She had seen it all before at her mother's funeral.

"So we have to support Melanie, and give her all the help we can."

"I know," Sadie whispered. "I should have tried before. I should have said something before it came to this."

"No one expected this."

Her father turned round worriedly as Melanie entered the room, wearing a plain black suit with a flower at the lapel. She said, "A white orchid. She always liked orchids. They were her favourite flowers."

Her husband nodded, but didn't say anything. He reached to touch her on the cheek, and brushed a strand of hair.

"You wear your smartest suit," Melanie said sadly, "to say goodbye to people."

Then she started crying, and Sadie crossed the room and cradled both of them in her trembling arms.

With one heart they all stood inside the quiet bedroom, finding how much loss hurts.

28

Eleanor was buried in a churchyard on a hill, where the wind blew from the moor. The sun shone out of a clear blue sky. Curlews out in the fields were singing haunting songs. Flowers strewn around the grave looked like the food of gods, carelessly tossed to earth.

In the vaulted doorway of the chapel mourners stood dressed in their Sunday best, white roses in their hands. The flowers would line the grave in which the corpse would lie in its white oak coffin.

They stood silently, unsure of what to do, unsure of when to move and how to drop their rose. Did they just throw it in, or did they say something, and who was meant to hear? So they waited patiently for someone to run them through their lines, like actors whistled in without rehearsal time.

"Sadie—" Martin appeared like a shadow from the trees around the grave. He had his suit on again and had plastered down his hair with a handful too much of gel. He was looking tense and pale, as pale as the slim white rose in Sadie's hand. "I just wanted to say that I'm very sorry Eleanor died this way," he said. "I know you weren't good friends, but it still must have been a shock. If there's anything I can do . . ."

She nodded and he glanced down. "I guess that's daft, really." He shuffled nervously as he glanced around the scene. He was trying hard to help, but there was nothing he could do. There was nothing Martin could say that would make the slightest difference to this day. "If you wanted to go and talk . . ." he said.

"Not today," Sadie whispered. "Maybe some other time."

"What about tomorrow then?"

"If you like." She didn't care. It was hard to think clearly with so much grief around.

29

Tony said, "Have you seen Dave yet?"

"He phoned me up," she said. "I told him we were through."

"How did he take that?"

"What could he do?" she asked. "I told him all about you, and that he was wasting his time."

"Did you meet him face to face?"

"No."

"I thought I saw you both in the coffee shop."

Sadie breathed a long sigh. "It must have been someone else." She wasn't in the mood for explaining things to him. Nor was she in the mood for facing one of Tony's jealous spates, so soon after the funeral. After a death, everything's different: the most important things seem less so and the very minor ones like nothing at all. Perspectives change.

She said, "He hasn't been near me, and I've stayed away from him. He just made one phone call, and that was all."

"Okay," Tony muttered. "I was just checking, Sade. It's no big deal, you know."

"Then why are you talking about it?" she said, then bit her lip. What was the point of having a useless fight? She just wanted to forget; she just wanted to get on with things; she didn't need any more grief.

"It's just that I don't like guys hanging around you, Sade. It gets me all knotted up, and I get tense inside."

"Then go and take a bath," she said, not caring much whether he hurt or not. It was getting too much now, this crowding in on her – people watching her every move, checking who she spoke to. What right had boys like this to think they had a say in who she chose to see?

She rose from the park bench, and said, "I'm going home."

"You've only just come out— "

"I'm going home again."

Tony looked alarmed. "We're not finished?" he said.

"Not if you'll give me a break," she said. She looked down sadly at his worried, suntanned face.

"You're always 'testing' me, seeing how far I'll go. There *isn't* anyone else; why can't you believe that?"

"I'm sorry, Sade," he said. "I get so jealous—"

"I know, it's *your* problem. Don't shift it on to me, because I need some breathing space. You can't drape me in chains like I'm a special pet who can't be let out alone."

"But it's other people who keep on crowding you—"

"No, Tony, it's you," she said. "You're the worst of all."

"I'm sorry, Sade," he said.

"Stop saying 'sorry'," she said. "It sounds pathetic."

Then she walked away and left him, wondering whether she'd gone too far. Wondering whether she cared at all in a grief-filled time like this, with people dead all around, physically and spiritually, and hands laying claim to her.

30

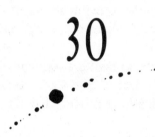

For some days afterwards Sadie kept a low profile, avoiding most people. She felt herself reeling from all the pressures in her life. Why couldn't people leave her alone and give her time and space to sort out where she was?

She tried talking to Melanie, hoping to patch things up, saying she would try harder to work their problems out. But Melanie was too withdrawn, too lost in her own grief to offer much comfort. Sadie's father seemed shell-shocked; a man who had suffered it all, only to have to suffer more. He had lost his first wife, and now his stepdaughter had followed her.

Why is there so much anguish? Sadie thought desperately. Why is there so much pain, and so few happy hearts? Why is there so much grief stalking the world? Which fool's responsible?

Sadie's father entered her room, touched her on the cheek, and said, "You've got a visitor."

"Who is it?" she asked as she sat up on the bed. "It's not that Martin Kemp? I can't face him right now."

He said, "It's someone from your school. She said her name's Tracey. She wants to talk to you."

Sadie let out a long moan. "I don't want to talk to *her*."

"She seems a bit upset; I think you should," he said. He touched her face again, and gently brushed her hair. "She brought some flowers for Melanie."

After a moment, Sadie wriggled off the bed and pulled some flat shoes on. She said, "She was Eleanor's friend; they got on well together. She never talks to me."

"Maybe she wants to this time," said her father. "Friendship hurts, particularly when one of you is the one who's left behind."

"She's probably come to ask if she can have some of Eleanor's things," Sadie said gloomily. She went downstairs, flicking her long hair back. She had no make-up on, and her clothes needed an iron. But sometimes other things get in the way of details like that, and feeling miserable's one of them.

"What do you want, Tracey?" she said as she pulled the lounge door shut, and leaned against a chair.

"I just wanted to talk to you," Tracey said quietly. She was looking washed-out too; grief affected everyone. She ran a hand through her hair, and threw a newspaper down. "Have you seen the ads in this?"

"Which ones?" said Sadie, though she knew full well.

"You know the ones I mean; I've heard you talking about them. Don't you think they're kind of odd, like somebody out there is playing games with us?"

"Why are they playing games with *you?*" said Sadie.

Tracey Scott gave a shrug. "They're having a dig at me because of all that 'angel' stuff. And they're having a dig at you too, because last night one message said, *'Hail the Kiss of Death'*."

Sadie watched her closely. "Why have you come here?"

"There's nowhere else to go; no one else would understand. We've never been that close, but maybe now's the time to try to patch things up."

Sadie considered this in silence for a time, then she offered Tracey a seat and sat down next to her. She said, "What do you want to do?"

"I don't know," Tracey said. "What can small

people do?" She took a tissue from her pocket, and gently blew her nose. "I haven't been out for days; I feel too scared to move."

"Me too," Sadie whispered. "I get so paranoid I can't trust anyone. Even my boyfriend's getting on my nerves."

"Your boyfriend's Tony Stern?"

"Yes." Sadie gave a nod.

"I went with him for a while. He's a really eerie boy; you ought to watch yourself."

"Why is he so eerie?" said Sadie curiously.

"Oh, just the things he does, the places he goes. He hangs around that house that's standing on the hill. He's quite obsessed with it."

Sadie said, "He told me he'd never been up there, but then I learned the truth. He'd been up there before – I think he's been with you."

"We went up several times," Tracey said, blowing her nose and wiping her reddened eyes. "He kept on 'chasing' me like he was Daniel Cross. He thought it was quite a game, pretending he had an axe. It's a really creepy place."

"I know, I've been up there," Sadie said quietly.

Tracey wiped her eyes again and put the tissue away. She was staring at the floor, as though she was mesmerized. She didn't seem much like the Tracey Sadie feared. She seemed quite helpless now. She said, "He often told me he has this constant dream that maybe Daniel Cross has been reborn in him. He says he feels his rage and he feels the kind of strength which ran through Daniel's arms. Don't you think that's really eerie?" she said, clutching Sadie's arm and staring into her eyes, as if to find some strength. "There's a kind of madness there; a hunger for the past; an urge to see it again."

Sadie said, "I've never seen this – he's never said this stuff. He just gets jealous sulks and wants to lock me up. He thinks being in love is such an intense thing it should block the whole world out."

Tracey gave a brief nod. "That's how it began," she said. "It starts with little things, then builds up more and more. It's like he wants to grab your soul and shut it in a box, and make you suffocate. There's just no freedom—"

Sadie said, "But he's cute."

"I know. That's the worst thing of all – you can't help liking him. It's like some kind of drug that's slowly killing you, but you keep going for more." Again Tracey gripped her, almost crushing Sadie's arm. "You have to take care, Sade; he's such a lethal boy. He gets under your skin and makes you all screwed up. I think he's dangerous."

So intense was the moment, and so real Tracey's fear, that Sadie felt herself choke inside and couldn't utter a word.

Was Tracey jealous of Sadie and trying to chase her off? Or was this a genuine warning?

31

They were in the empty coffee shop and it was approaching closing time when Sadie had it out with Tony.

"Have you been lying to me?" she said.

"About what?" Tony said.

"About nearly everything," she said, watching his eyes. "About that spooky house; about you and Tracey Scott; about you and me, probably."

Tony looked astonished. "What are you talking about?"

Sadie put her Coke glass down, and slid it to one side. Then she leaned over the cloth, which was a white damask, well-frayed through constant use. She said, "Well, according to Tracey you almost killed yourself when she stopped going out with you, because you were so upset. And as for that old house, you spend so much time up there you're practically *living* there. Which isn't quite the same, really, as saying that you didn't like her, and that you've been to that house – what? No more than three times. She says you're obsessed with the place, and have this crazy thing about being Daniel reborn."

Tony started laughing. "That's just absurd," he said. "I've never said anything to make her think like that. She's only winding you up – it's just a jealous thing because she's ticked off with me."

"Why should she be ticked off with you?" Sadie asked cautiously, her eyes narrow slits in the tense mask of her face.

"Just because I'm going with you and she wants to screw things up. She's a jealous kind of girl."

Tony stared at her innocently from behind his glass of Coke, and Sadie watched his eyes, looking for hidden signs. "She says you're the jealous one."

He gave a diffident shrug. "That's just her talking. I was never that keen on her and it probably hurt her pride; no doubt it would suit her fine to see us falling out. Tracey can't bear to think that there's someone in the world who won't go mad for her." He leaned forward suddenly, and clasped his hands. His eyes were grave and calm as he sought for words. "I might have bent the truth, but that isn't the same as telling you lies. I only wanted it to *seem* like I'd never been up there before, so that when we went together it would be a special thing. A kind of romantic trip, like lovers stepping out to explore things side by side."

"But you're always lying to me," said Sadie.

"No. I'm not. I lied over two small things, and they're hardly lies at all."

"They are to me," she said. "I never tell you lies."

"Well, aren't you perfect?" Tony turned away angrily, tapping the side of his glass. He stared out at the street, trying to avoid her face.

Sadie said, "I don't like deceit."

"Well, go and find a saint," he muttered moodily.

32

Sadie went out with Martin Kemp for no better reason than to pay Tony back. When her lips kissed Martin's they did so without love or pride, and although she didn't feel good about this she felt justified. She thought that liars and cheats should get their just desserts, even if vengeance sometimes hurts.

In her defence it could at least be said that though she didn't love Martin, Sadie *did* care about him. She made it plain to him right from the start that this wasn't going to last, and he seemed to accept that. It might have been just to please her, in the hope that she would change her mind, but for a time at least they both had what they craved.

In fact, as time went on Sadie began to think

that Martin wasn't too bad after all. He was always very respectful and kind to her, he had no jealous moods and never told blatant lies. After her last affair, it was a great relief to be able to relax.

Always hanging over her, though, were the names "Tony" and "Dave", and she couldn't forget those eerie personal ads. She found it hard to understand why they hadn't been stopped, and she often talked about them. She said they were a definite warning that she was on the killer's list, and that she shouldn't be left alone in case the killer struck. She wanted more and more for her dad or Melanie to be watching over her.

"Sadie," her father said, "there's a policeman in the hall. He wants to talk to you."

"Okay," she murmured, as she flicked her long hair back and hurried down the stairs. She found no one in the hall, but through the kitchen door, she could hear voices. Someone was talking, laughing, clinking a cup. Someone was saying something about how hot it was. As she peered inside the room she saw a grey-haired man holding a coffee cup.

"You must be Sadie."

She nodded, but didn't speak.

"My name's Inspector Sharpe. Come on – come in, sit down."

She walked in cautiously, and sat down on a chair near Melanie.

She said, "What do you want to talk about?"

"Oh, just a general chat. How do you feel, Sadie? You've been through a difficult time."

"I'm not too bad," she said, watching with wary eyes as he smiled at her. "It's not been easy."

"No, I'm sure it's not," he said. "Three murders – all your friends."

"Two weren't friends of mine."

"All the same it must have been quite a shock."

"You don't expect these things."

"Of course not," he replied. He sipped his coffee and watched her pleasantly. He had an open face, as if he possessed no guile. His eyes were corn-flower blue, and so big and bright they made him look almost like a child. "One was your sister. Did you two get along?"

Sadie chewed her lip. "Not that well," she replied.

"Hard when a step-sister's thrust into your life. Did you feel jealous of her?"

"Not exactly jealous; we just never quite got along."

"You felt a bit pushed out, I should imagine." His blue eyes smiled.

Sadie shrugged. "I don't know. I suppose it's hard sometimes. Sometimes everything's hard."

The inspector nodded gravely, as if he under-stood. He took a pale Rich Tea and dunked it in his mug, catching it on his tongue just before it broke in half. He seemed to be quite at ease.

"So we've had three murders, and we have no suspect. We follow every lead, but it brings us out nowhere. The only clue we have is those strange personal ads – you know the ones I mean?"

Sadie nodded nervously.

"I think it would help a lot –" The inspector dunked again, and finished his biscuit off – "if we knew why they were sent and who the sender was. That makes sense, doesn't it?"

Again Sadie nodded.

"What do you think they mean?"

"I've no idea," she said. "Why are you asking me?"

"Because I've tracked them down and found where they come from. *You* sent them in, Sadie."

Sadie stared at Inspector Sharpe in the silence of the room.

"Did you send them, Sadie?"

She nodded. "How did you know?" she asked.

"One of the things we checked was the records at your school. We compared handwriting – we check lots of things when we're hunting down clues. It wasn't actually very easy because you'd changed your style, but every now and then you kept on lapsing back."

"I tried to do my best."

"I know. Everyone does." He smiled half sadly. "Why did you send them?"

"Because I was scared," she said. "No one would listen to me; and I felt I had to do something. It was that message on the wall – I thought it was meant for me; I've seen the Angel of Death. I thought it might be Tracey, or even Eleanor. I thought they were planting phoney clues, when they were really after me. Neither one liked me much, and both had a good reason to kill Maurice Cope. We all had a reason; he was a very horrid boy. If it hadn't been for that wall I wouldn't have thought much of it. But the sign – *The Angel Walks* – I thought that was meant for me. It seemed personal to me."

"So you sent your own messages—"

"To make people sit up. I thought you'd have to look if you thought there might be more, and you'd find who the killer was. It seems odd that the one I suspected turned out to be a victim."

The inspector didn't move as Sadie rattled off her words, and when she had finished he lowered his cup slowly and ran his hands through his hair. His face creased in a frown. "Are you seeing a doctor, Sadie?"

She said, "A psychiatrist."

He nodded. "Yes, I'd heard. Would you tell me why that is?"

"I have some nasty dreams."

"And you felt you'd been shut out?"

"I suppose so."

"And those personal ads – they were a bid for attention? Some kind of protest?"

"I suppose so," she said weakly. "It all seems stupid now. It makes *me* look stupid."

"Not stupid," the inspector said, "but very close to it. It wasn't exactly clever. Why didn't you come to us with this?"

"I thought you'd laugh at me."

"We wasted a lot of time trying to sort this out."

"I'm sorry," Sadie said.

"Why did you feel so scared?"

"Mostly because of my dreams. Have you ever had them – the dreams that wake you up and you're covered with sweat and trying to scream for help?"

"Not often," the inspector said.

"They're really awful things."

"I can imagine," he replied. After that he just looked at her, uncertain what to do. Then he looked at Melanie, and finally at Sadie's dad. He said, "I'll leave it with you to sort this business out. I've got no further questions here."

For a long time there was silence in the room, and then her father spoke. He said, "Why didn't you say something?"

"I tried to," Sadie whispered. "I tried to tell you all, but no one listened to me. Everyone was too busy dealing with other things to spare any time for me."

Her father looked anguished. "That isn't true, Sadie. I've always got time for you—"

"It didn't seem that way. I seemed to be all alone, frightened and under threat. I feel so scared sometimes." Sadie gazed up tearfully. "Why does everyone come after me? Why is everyone always leaning on me, putting pressure on me? Why can't they just leave me alone?"

33

Sadie climbed the hill overlooking her home. She had made a fool of herself in front of her family and the police. Even if nobody else ever found this out, Sadie knew it herself. She would have to come to terms with the fact that the police considered her a childish time-waster, a little spoiled-brat girl who cried "Wolf!" every time she saw a dog.

What made it so painful was that she could see their point: it *was* a childish prank which deserved to be found out. On the brink of adulthood, with her life laid out ahead, she seemed almost intent on retreating into a shell. Maybe it was a fear of growing up. Maybe it was a fear of staying young. Who knows?

* * *

"Penny for your thoughts."

Martin must have followed her, faithful as a pet dog.

His thin shadow fell over Sadie as she glanced up from a seat formed by a slab of rock which had warmed in the afternoon sun. She shaded her eyes, squinting like a mole caught unawares. She said, "That's the third time you've said that; don't you get tired of it?"

He sat down at her side, and took hold of her hand. "I never get tired of you." He pulled out a tuft of grass and handed it to her. "Sometimes I want to know all of you and read all your thoughts."

"I doubt you'd learn much; they're mostly simple things." Sadie leaned against his arm and let her head subside on to his shoulder.

They sat like that for a long time, watching the town below. It looked so peaceful now, it was hard to believe that it was a murky place where nightmare shadows lurked; a place where every home, every school, every shop, was conscious of murder.

She said, "Do you ever feel you want to go away from here, and start all over again? Go to some different town where no one knows your name? Find a place without fear?"

"I don't know," said Martin. "I kind of like it here."

"I don't," Sadie murmured. "I'm frightened by

the place. What if one of us is next? What if the Angel comes and brings death on her wings?"

"Then I'll protect you," Martin said, holding her tight. "I'll fight off all the demons in this town."

"That might not be enough," she said, squeezing his arm.

34

Tony wasn't prepared to let his girlfriend go without some kind of a fight. A string of letters arrived at Sadie's house, each more venomous than the one before. He tried pleading, cajoling, reasoning, and then he threatened her. She showed the letters to Martin, who thought Tony must be insane. He said that no normal boy would write letters like that. Sadie said, "Keep out of his way."

"I'm not afraid of him."

"You should be," Sadie said. "I never realized how much hatred he feels. He must hate everyone and everything."

"Maybe we should go to the police."

Sadie gave a short laugh. "I'm sure they'd go for

that: saying my ex-boyfriend's not very pleased with me."

"But they might warn him off," Martin said earnestly. "He needs some warning off."

Sadie folded the letters and shoved them into her bag. She said, "They might just make him mad and he might come after me. I'll handle this myself." She tossed her long hair back, and her face looked resolute.

"I could have a word with him."

"No, Martin, I'll do that." She touched him on the arm and smiled into his eyes. "I know you're very sweet and brave and all that, but I can handle this."

"Don't get him mad, though," he said, looking concerned. "You don't know what he's like if he loses control."

"No, I won't get him mad. I'll just tell him to stop writing or I *will* go to the police." She picked her bag up and slung it over her arm. "I'll go and see him now and get it over with. I'll meet you later on and let you know how it went. Wish me luck," she said.

He kissed her, then said, "You take good care."

"I will. I can't see him murdering *me*!" She was trying to make a joke, but her eyes betrayed the tension she felt inside. She had sensed a viciousness underlying Tony's words. She could see what

Tracey meant when she said that Tony Stern might well be dangerous.

"I didn't send them," he said. "It wasn't me, Sade."

"Don't be ridiculous."

"That's not my handwriting; mine's nothing like that. That stuff's all over the place, and I've got very neat writing. I'll show you some if you like."

Puzzled, Sadie looked down at the letters in her hand. "So if they're not from you, who *are* they from?" she asked.

"I don't know. Someone's just using me to frighten you." He read the letters again then handed them back to her. "Somebody hates you, Sade."

Sadie looked round despairingly. She didn't know what to do, where to go or what to say. She was out of ideas.

Tony went on. "I thought of writing, but I didn't know what to say. I thought that if you knew me at all you would already know how I felt. I was really crazy about you. I still am," he said. "I really miss you, Sade."

But Sadie was too distracted to take this in. "I really need to know who sent this stuff," she said. "How did they know about you? How did they know the things to *put* in the letters?"

Tony gave a brief shrug. "Maybe they've been watching us. I saw David sometimes when we were on a date."

"David was watching us? I don't believe that," she said. "He isn't *that* stupid."

"Well, who then?" asked Tony. "Who could hate you that much? Who would go out of their way to find out all this stuff?"

"I don't know," Sadie said. "But I'm going to find out who and put a stop to it."

She would do it if she could, but where did she begin?

"Why did you lie to me?"

"Because I'm a fool," he said, handing her a red rose.

A few moments after she got back to the house, there was a knock at the door. It was David. He had a smile on his face and was holding out some flowers. Sadie was still clutching Tony's rose.

"I thought you might like these to cheer you up," he said.

Sadie couldn't believe it. She'd had enough today without coping with Dave. She didn't take the flowers or even look at him. "Just go away," she sighed.

"These are a peace offering!" David wouldn't take the hint. He seemed oblivious to the expression in her eyes.

"Thanks very much," she said. "I don't want a peace offering. I don't want anything."

"But these are roses—"

Sadie held out her hand. "I've got a red rose here; I don't need any more."

"But there are twelve of them!"

"Please go away," she sighed. "I'm too worn out to talk."

This time David looked a little crestfallen. Shadows filled his eyes. "You see those other guys—"

"What other guys?" she said. "Oh, David, go away! I don't need this right now."

David took a step back as he saw her anger flare. All of a sudden the bunch of flowers seemed heavy. "What's up with *you*?" he said.

"Don't talk to me like that!" She glared into his eyes, outraged. What right did David have to say something like that? She'd never asked him round; she'd never invited him to turn up with some flowers!

But he stood defiantly, with one foot in the porch. "I'd merely like to know what makes those two so good."

"Maybe I *like* them, Dave."

"I'm better than them," he said. "I can make you happy, if you'll just let me try."

"Maybe I don't want you to," she said. "Have you ever thought of that?"

"Well, yes . . ." David frowned. He seemed genuinely puzzled that Sadie could prefer Tony and Martin to him. Sure, he'd gone away for a while, but now he was back again. What was so wrong with her?

"You know, you're wasting yourself on stupid jerks like that."

"And who the heck are *you* to talk?" she shouted through the porch. She was about to close the door, but he had wedged his foot in it, like a nuisance salesman. "You must think I'm stupid!"

"You liked me once. In fact, as I recall, you couldn't get enough of me. You can't have changed that much. You don't have to be scared. I'll forgive you your little sins."

"*Have you gone crazy?*" She wrestled with the door. She tried to kick his foot away, and he pulled back. He was still holding out the flowers, as if ignoring all that was going on around him.

"Shall I call another time?"

"Don't bother!" Sadie yelled as she finally slammed the door and left him on the drive.

"What was all that about?" her father said.

"Who knows?" Sadie panted. "I'm losing track these days."

35

Soon after, the family took a break. They went to the Lake District, to a cottage near Troutbeck, where they hoped the country air would help them forget all the death and grief they had left behind. Things did indeed look promising, for it was a lovely spot overlooked by rolling hills and sheep with placid eyes. It seemed the kind of place where peace could be assured, if they ever got the water to work . . .

"There's something wrong with it," said Melanie, as she kicked the ancient water pipe. "There's nothing happening, except a groaning sound."

"It takes a while to come through – it says so in the book."

"Longer than half an hour?" Melanie said, frowning at Sadie's father.

He put his book down. "Have I got to go outside and start groping around?"

"I'll go," Sadie offered, glad to be far away from her normal routine. She felt exhilarated to be in the country air; to hear the curlews cry and see the swallows swoop. It was heaven on earth after the recent weeks of strain and misery.

Pulling her shoes on she ran out to the yard, where she saw a ginger cat watching her from a wall. The cat came with the house, and treated all strangers with equanimity. As she struggled with the pump it rubbed round her legs, as though offering her advice.

When it had grown bored with that the cat wandered into the house and sat on Sadie's bed, staring out at the hills. It seemed to lack only the means of putting across its thoughts in human form.

That evening, around a smouldering log fire, playing poker for sweets, they all agreed that the holiday had been a great idea.

"Maybe we should move up here," said Sadie, cheating hard but not as successfully as her father, who had played for years. "We've had nothing but unhappiness; maybe we ought to move away and start again. I mean just the three of us . . ." She looked at her father and Melanie. They were a family now, brought close by Eleanor's death. Out of the fires of grief a phoenix had been born, and was spreading its wings.

"I've got a job, Sade. I can't just give it up." Her father looked around for the missing ace of spades. He had shoved it up his sleeve, but somehow it had gone, and he thought Sadie was sitting on it. "It's not that easy."

"Why not?"

Melanie agreed with Sadie. "We've been through a terrible time, so why not make a change? Find somewhere nice to live, set up your own business – you're very capable."

Sadie's father grunted. He didn't sound convinced. "I've been with that firm for years."

"Oh, don't be such a wimp." Sadie produced the ace and scooped up all the sweets. "We can do anything."

Sadie really felt it; she felt it in her bones. She felt it when she went outside alone later that night. There was an entire world out there, and a brilliant, endless sky. There were a million stars just for her.

36

For two days Sadie walked among the empty hills, running down rocky slopes with a sense of complete liberation. She explored the nearby towns, and bought some Lakeland slate for no reason at all, other than that she liked the shape.

From a windswept hilltop she looked down on a world devoid of jealous boys, wild rages and sudden death. She thought that never again would she find such a perfect spot in which to cleanse her soul.

Every breath was intoxicating, every footstep was a joy. Every startled, running sheep was a delight and a charm. When she saw a swooping hawk she thought it was a sign that she had been freed at last.

She could spread her own wings and plummet through a void which once had threatened her with gloom for ever more. She could rise beyond the gloom; she could rise up to the stars; she was free as a bird.

"Are you having a good time here?" said her father.

"Wonderful!" Sadie said breathlessly. "It's like a new world waiting to be explored. No boys coming around with bunches of dead flowers; no girls like Tracey Scott; no nightmares in the dark; no terrors round the bend." She wanted to scream out for the relief she felt inside. She hugged her father close, and said, "It's like old times. Just the three of us, nobody else around—"

"The water's off again."

"Oh, not again!" she cried. "I haven't got to go outside?"

Her father said, "I thought you liked pumping. I thought that was your job?"

"Yes, that was yesterday," she said. "It's boring now." As she pulled her sandals on she looked round for the cat. It usually appeared when she went to the door. "What's happened to the cat?"

"He's probably off somewhere, hunting down rats and things."

She said, "I hope he keeps them outside; we don't want rats in here."

"And you the country girl who wants to live round here!"

"I didn't know there were rats," she said, pulling a face. "I don't mind sheep and things."

She hurried outside to prime the ancient pump, but pulled up some way short as a movement caught her eye. It was a bird across the lawn, hopping uncertainly around an orange shape. As Sadie approached it, her father came outside. He said, "What's that thing there?"

Sadie said, "It's the cat."

Someone had shot the beast. There were puncture-wounds in its fur where air-gun pellets had hit.

37

The next day a letter came, addressed to "Sadie Ross". Sadie stared at it.

"Nobody knows where I am," she said. "I didn't tell anyone."

Her father gave a shrug. "It's addressed to you."

She opened the envelope with trembling hands. Inside was a plain, hand-written card. It read: *I know you're there. The Angel knows it all.*

She crushed the card in her hands and stared at her father.

"They know I'm here," she sighed.

They loaded up the car and headed straight back home before anything else could go wrong. The whole adventure had suddenly turned sour on them. Fear had not given up on them at all, it had merely paused for breath. When it felt suitably refreshed it had hunted them and found out where they were.

As they drove down the motorway, leaving the Lakes behind, they learned what torture is – not a sudden pain, but the repetition of pain, the remorselessness of it.

Sadie said, "No one knew, though, – no one knew where we were. I never told anyone—"

"You must have told someone." Her father dropped a gear to overtake a truck, then swung out recklessly.

"I *didn't*," said Sadie. "I didn't know myself until we got up here exactly where we were going. I knew the Lake District, but not the house address. How could I have told anyone?"

Her father grunted. "Well, try to think," he said. "Because someone up there just went and killed a cat. That Martin Kemp once shot a few of them, as I recall."

"I don't think it was Martin, though I don't know why," she said. "But I wondered about David – if he could have found out I think he'd been following me to see who I've been with. He could have followed us."

"All the way up the motorway?"

"How do I know?" Sadie said, staring out at the fields which were now flashing by. "Someone must

154

have followed us; they'd hardly pick Troutbeck on the off-chance."

"Well, we're going straight to the police as soon as we get home," he said. "I want to stop this now before it gets out of hand. You can't have lunatics chasing you all over the place, shooting at people's pets."

As silence descended, Sadie wound her window down and took a last, deep breath of the cleansing country air. After this it was back to school, back to streets haunted by fear. Back to the firing line.

38

"Well, we'll do the best we can, but we don't hold out too much hope," Inspector Sharpe murmured. "Typewritten letters are notoriously difficult to trace."

"But no one knew we were there," said Sadie's father grimly.

The inspector said, "I hate to point this out, but that's not much help, as you can probably see." He turned to Sadie, who was sitting on his desk, her hands tucked underneath her thighs, in a stiff, defensive pose. He said, "So you think this David Grant may have followed you up there, and found out where you were staying?"

Sadie couldn't be too certain. "It's possible," she said.

"Why should he want to do that? Why should he threaten you?"

"I don't know," Sadie said. "Jealousy possibly. Just trying to hurt me."

"Because you ditched him?"

"I don't know," Sadie said. "You'd have to ask him that; I don't know what's in his mind. All I know is that he came round to the house not long before we went away and started acting strange, then he became threatening."

The inspector nodded and leaned back in his chair. He toyed with a slim black pen and watched Sadie's eyes. He was trying to read her thoughts, to see if she knew any more than she was telling him.

"You said he's in love with you."

"He said so," Sadie said.

"It's a funny kind of way of demonstrating love. I don't suppose you brought the cat?"

Sadie looked horrified. "Of course not! We buried it!"

The inspector grunted. "That's a pity," he murmured. "We might have learned something. But at least you're all okay."

"Not like the cat," said Sadie.

"No, the cat's not so good."

Reaching behind him, the inspector pulled a cord to adjust the venetian blinds which were letting sunlight slant in. Her father wished he was playing golf instead of talking death on a bright, hot day like this.

"Your other boyfriends – Tony Stern and Martin Kemp. Could they have followed you?"

"Not unless they ran," she said. "They haven't got cars."

He nodded and made a note. "But David has a car?"

Sadie gave a short nod. "A lime-green Peugeot thing."

"But you never saw the car while you were in the Lakes?"

"It's a fairly remote spot; all we saw were ramblers and sheep and jackdaws."

"Well, I can have a word with him and try to warn him off, although even if he sent the note there's not much we can do. He's made no threats in it, and it's no crime to send someone a letter. If he actually threatens you, technically that's an assault, although not the easiest of things to prove in court. I suggest you go back home and have another think about who you might have told about your holiday." He put his pen down and stared at Sadie and her father. "Sometimes these things come back – something that slipped your mind. Meanwhile I'll talk to David Grant."

"That might just make things worse."

"There's not much else I can do."

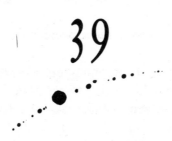

39

"So you ran off to the police because you thought I threatened you. Who do you think I am?"

"You keep away from me," Sadie said, backing against a fence which ran along the track a short distance from her home. It was a place where lovers walked, and hedgehogs rustled leaves on starlit evenings. But there was no starlight on the night David appeared. There were no lovers there, no hedgehogs in the grass. There was only Sadie Ross and a young man with blazing eyes.

"What did you think I'd do?" he asked. "Go mad like Martin Kemp? Go killing innocent things and sending out creepy notes? I'm not a nut, Sadie; not like your other friends—"

"Leave me alone, David." She shuffled sideways, trying to get past the arm which he'd braced against the fence, as an obstacle in her path. But David wasn't going to move until he'd finished.

"I'm not a fool, you know – I know what's going on."

"What?" Sadie almost winced, as though he might lash out.

"Three people dropping dead – three people Sadie Ross would be glad to see gone."

"What are you talking about? I haven't killed anyone!"

"No. Maybe Tony did, or even Martin Kemp. Maybe you asked them to, or maybe they're just trying to show how 'loyal' they are to you."

"Have you gone crazy?" Sadie said, horrified. "Those boys might like me, Dave, but they're not going to kill for me. Good grief! They're not that crazy about me—"

"No?" David leaned towards her. "I think you're wonderful, and I'm really mad about you. I'd kill someone myself if it helped to make you mine. I'd even kill myself if that's what you want. I really love you, Sade."

Sadie stared dumbstruck at the flame in David's eyes: a flame of worship, lust, and dark, obsessive love. If it got out of control it could go crazy and kill the one it loved, mistaking jealous rage for a sense of grievous hurt. It might come to believe that if it could not have her, then nor should anyone else.

"I really love you," he said, as gloom fell on the track from the thickening clouds above. "I can't live without you. I can't live with the thought that you've found someone else." His fingertips touched her cheek, like an elf's breath. "Can you understand that, Sade? Do you know how much it hurts? It's like an awful pain that tears you up inside. It makes you *mad* with love."

Sadie said, "But I don't love you—"

"I know," he said sadly. "That's the most awful thing – I know you never will. And that's okay for you, but how will I survive knowing you're in the world? Who can I turn to when the ache becomes too strong? Who's going to hold my hand when I wake up in the night? Who's going to call my name when I'm lost and all alone? Who's going to *love* me, Sade?"

Sadie didn't have to answer, because he turned away and strode off down the track, vanishing into the gloom. It was probably just as well, because she wouldn't have known what to say. She could only watch him until he disappeared, and wonder why it is that love brings jealous rage. Jealousy is not a gift, a boon or a compliment; it is the world's great curse.

40

The pressures on Sadie were now even stronger than before. From every quarter, it seemed, people were crowding her – people with jealous hearts and cynical, selfish thoughts. Their minds were filled with greed; the smiles which touched their eyes were dark, sinister things.

How could she trust them when they were watching her every move, questioning her every word. She felt she had no space to turn around. Somebody, somewhere, was watching her . . .

"Sadie? Are you all right in there?"

"I'm okay," she replied, and her father walked away.

She was in her bedroom, looking out on a starlit

sky. Thin clouds covered the moon, like gauze dropped by the night. She held a small white candle, its yellow flame dancing nervously, reflecting in her sombre eyes.

"Martin, I've got something which will help us name the killer. I need your help," she said.

She could hear his breathing, like a whisper down the phone. "Go to the police," he said.

"I can't," Sadie murmured. "I've been to them before. They think I'm just a fool trying to prove something. They won't believe me—"

"What do you want *me* to do?"

"I need you for support, in case something goes wrong."

"I won't be much support."

"You'll do just fine, Martin. It won't be dangerous. I just want to see someone – the killer – then we can go to the police and have him locked away."

"See who?"

"Martin, I don't know yet. We have to go somewhere."

"Go where?" asked Martin.

"To the old house on the hill."

"Not the old madman's house? I really hate that place. Can't we go somewhere else?"

"No, that's the place they've picked."

"*They've* picked? What's going on?"

There was a long pause, then Sadie said, "Trust me. I'll tell you later on if you'll agree to come."

"I'm not sure . . ."

"Meet me at nine o'clock."

She sensed his heart plummet.

41

She met him in the lane which curved around the hill leading up to the house. The sky was stormy, and clouds sped from the west. The sun was sinking fast inside a veil of mist. Thin drops of slanting rain were falling like the tears of angry, swindled gods.

Not far above them the old house creaked and groaned. Doors banged against their frames, shutters opened and closed. Thick, sinister shadows fell on the ground around. Windows made watchful eyes.

Sadie climbed off her bike and walked across the grass to where Martin waited. He watched her warily, doubtfully. Daylight was fading fast and twilight filled his eyes, so that they looked quite black. He gripped a long torch, which he held more like a club, as though prepared to fight if he had to. He didn't say anything as she gazed into his face and smiled.

"I had a note," she said. "Shoved through the door last night. It said to meet them here."

"Meet who?" asked Martin.

"The killer," Sadie said. She gave him the note, and he held it close to his eyes. He could barely make it out in the deep and bruise-like shade which spread across the hill.

"Who's it from?" he murmured.

"I don't know," Sadie said. "That's what we're doing here; trying to find out."

The note said: *Sadie's fate will be decided tonight in the old house on the hill. Be there at midnight, and be sure to come alone. I shall be watching you, just as I always watch. I have watched you for years – I'll watch for ever more.* It was signed, *The Angel.*

"It isn't midnight."

"I'm not stupid," she said. "I want to be there first. I want to check the place to see if there are any clues, and then we'll lie in wait until the killer comes. As soon as we've seen their face we'll run off to the police, and tell them who it is. We'll have the note for evidence—"

"You should give it to them now."

"The police don't trust me much when it comes to creepy notes. This is the best chance we've got.

We have to know ourselves. We have to know for sure."

Martin took a deep breath as he handed back the note, and slowly shook his head, from doubt more than despair. "We're really playing with fire."

"I'll save you if you save me." Her jokey remark failed to lift the mood – the tension she felt showed through in every word. She didn't try to smile any more.

"What do you think?" she asked quietly.

"I've told you what I think."

"But will you come with me?" she said, touching his hand.

"We could just wait out here. We could hide behind that wall—"

"They'd see us," Sadie said. "It's all too open. The only secret place is deep inside that house, hidden in one of the rooms. Once we know who the killer is we'll sneak off out the back. We'll lose them in the dark."

Martin stayed silent, looking lonely and lost. His eyes stared into hers, pleading without a sound.

Sadie said, "We can put an end to this. Trust me."

Martin sighed.

42

They forced the heavy door back and stepped into the gloom which filled the hallway. The torchlight chased shadows away, but as soon as it moved on they reappeared.

As they crept forward echoes ran through the house, and every heartbeat was like a booming drum. They could not draw a breath without sending a thread of whisper through the air.

Martin said, "They'll hear us."

"I doubt they'll be here yet."

"I've got less faith than you."

"Let's check the rooms quickly."

Martin aimed the torch upstairs, and faced a greater dark than he had ever seen.

They went from floor to floor, checking out

every patch of shadow, every room. They heard strange whispers as the house turned in its sleep. They startled sleeping birds which were roosting in the porch. They frightened off a rat, but nobody appeared, killer or otherwise. They were the only source of light, the only touch of warmth, the only scent of flesh.

"There's just the cellar left," Sadie said, looking down the ink-pool stairwell. "Daniel Cross hid there when he was plotting to kill his wife. That's where he kept his axe—"

"Shut up!" Martin whispered.

"We'll have to go and look. We'll have to check it out."

"This is too weird by half. Why don't we clear out of here while we've still got the strength to run?"

"Because they'll hunt me out. I'm next on their list. Why else would they send the note? I'll go if you're afraid—"

"No, I'll go," Martin said. It was the curse of chivalry which made him offer himself, but he yearned with all his heart for her to come as well –

"I'll come down right behind."

Martin eased out his breath. "You hold the torch," he sighed.

Martin crept down the stairs while Sadie aimed the

torch over his shoulder. As he reached the cellar floor he said, "Someone's been here. There are footsteps in the dirt, and someone's dragged something—"

Sadie said, "Look around, but don't spend too much time. Let's climb back out of here." The silence of the room was deeper than a tomb. Every nerve, every thread of fibre in her being wanted to back away.

Martin said, "There's someone down here! It looks like David Grant!"

"What?" Sadie backed away towards the cellar door.

"It's David. All beat up – he's tied up with a rope. Bring the torch here, Sadie."

But as Martin looked up he saw Sadie disappear, then the heavy door closed and a bolt slid into place. The last thing he heard was her footsteps fading into the distance.

43

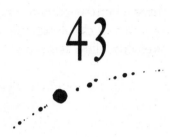

Martin pounded the door as Sadie quietly performed her final task. She left the old house and walked round to a shed, where she grabbed a can of petrol she'd stored there. She dragged it through the grass all the way to the porch, then up into the hall.

Wrenching the cap off, she tipped the petrol out, sending it across the floor in a spreading rainbow pool. It flowed under the cellar door and trickled down the stairs.

"What are you doing, Sade?" Martin cried.

She took a length of wood, wrapped a rag round it and soaked it in the fuel. Then she walked to the front door, and lit a long brown match, and set fire to the rag.

As Martin's screams rose she tossed the rag inside the hall and the petrol caught light with a sudden rush. A wave of orange flame went tearing through the hall and touched the cellar door.

"Sadie!" Martin screamed as she slowly walked away, and sat down on the grass to watch the old house burn. It didn't take long: the house was tinder dry. It went up like a flare.

44

Sadie was still sitting on the grass, almost mesmerized by the orange, dancing light, as the police cars roared and wailed their way up the dark hill. The heat which touched her face went straight to her soul. She felt such peace inside; such relief and such joy that her work was almost done. Once she had killed Tony and Tracey there would be no one left to meddle with her life and make her unhappy. She would be left all alone – just her and her family: her dad and Melanie.

She had never been comfortable with people crowding her, people in her way, people who put her down. Soon there would be no more of that because they'd all be dead. But she'd still be alive.

The police would never catch her. They would

never dare to dream that she'd do such a thing. She was too clever for them.

She was still saying that when they eased her into a car.

"They won't catch me," she smiled . . .

Point

Pointing the way forward

More compelling reading from top authors.

The Highest Form of Killing
Malcolm Rose
Death is in the very air . . .

Seventeenth Summer
K.M. Peyton
*Patrick Pennington – mean, moody and out
of control . . .*

Secret Lives
William Taylor
*Two people drawn together by their mysterious
pasts . . .*

Flight 116 is Down
Caroline B. Cooney
Countdown to disaster . . .

Forbidden
Caroline B. Cooney
Theirs was a love that could never be . . .

Hostilities
Caroline Macdonald
*In which the everyday throws shadows of another,
more mysterious world . . .*

POINT FANTASY

Read Point Fantasy and escape into the realms of the imagination; the kingdoms of mortal and immortal elements. Lose yourself in the world of the dragon and the dark lord, the princess and the mage; a world where magic rules and the forces of evil are ever poised to attack . . .

Available now:

POINT FANTASY

Foiling the Dragon
Susan Price
What will become of Paul Welsh, pub poet,
when he meets a dragon – with a passion for
poetry, and an appetite for poets . . .

Dragonsbane
Patricia C. Wrede
Princess Cimorene discovers that living with a
dragon is not always easy, and there is a
serious threat at hand . . .

The Webbed Hand
Jenny Jones
Princess Maria is Soprafini's only hope
against the evil Prince Ferrian and his
monstrous Fireflies . . .

Look out for:
Daine the Hunter:
Book 3: The Emperor Mage
Tamora Price

Star Warriors
Peter Beere

The "Renegades" Series
Book 3: The Return of the Wizard
Jessica Palmer

Elf-King
Susan Price

Point Horror

Are you hooked on horror? Are you thrilled by fear? Then these are the books for you. A powerful series of horror fiction designed to keep you quaking in your shoes.

The Watcher
Lael Littke

Dream Date
The Waitress
by Sinclair Smith

The Phantom
by Barbara Steiner

The Baby-sitter
The Baby-sitter II
The Baby-sitter III
Beach House
Beach Party
The Boyfriend
Call Waiting
The Dead Girlfriend
The Girlfriend
Halloween Night
The Hitchhiker
Hit and Run
The Snowman
by R.L. Stine

Thirteen
by Christopher Pike, R.L. Stine and others
Thirteen More Tales of Horror
by Diane Hoh and others

Look out for:

The Diary
Sinclair Smith

Twins
Caroline B. Cooney

The Yearbook
Peter Lerangis

The Witness
R.L. Stine

Point Romance

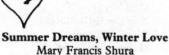

If you like Point Horror, you'll love Point Romance!

Anyone can hear the language of love.

**Are you burning with passion, and aching with desire?
Then these are the books for you! Point Romance brings
you passion, romance, heartache . . . and *love*.**

Point Romance

Caroline B. Cooney

The lives, loves and hopes of five young girls appear in this dazzling mini series:

Anne – coming to terms with a terrible secret that has changed her whole life.

Kip – everyone's best friend, but no one's dream date . . . why can't she find the right guy?

Molly – out for revenge against the four girls she has always been jealous of . . .

Emily – whose secure and happy life is about to be threatened by disaster.

Beth Rose – dreaming of love but wondering if it will ever become a reality.

Follow the five through their last years of high school, in four brilliant titles: *Saturday Night, Last Dance, New Year's Eve,* and *Summer Nights*

The Obernewtyn Chronicles:
Book 1: Obernewtyn
Book 2: The Farseekers
Isobelle Carmody
A new breed of humans are born into a hostile world
struggling back from the brink of apocalypse . . .

Random Factor
Jessica Palmer
Battle rages in space. War has been erased from earth and is
now controlled by an all-powerful computer – until a random
factor enters the system . . .

First Contact
Nigel Robinson
In 1992 mankind launched the search for extra-terrestrial
intelligence. Two hundred years later, someone responded . . .

Virus
Molly Brown
A mysterious virus is attacking the staff of an engineering plant
. . . Who, or *what* is responsible?

Look out for:

Strange Orbit
Margaret Simpson

Scatterlings
Isobelle Carmody

Body Snatchers
Stan Nicholls

Read Point SF and enter a new dimension . . .

THE UNDERWORLD TRILOGY
Peter Beere

When life became impossible for the homeless of London many left the streets to live beneath the earth. They made their homes in the corridors and caves of the Underground. They gave their home a name. They called it UNDERWORLD.

UNDERWORLD
It was hard for Sarah to remember how long she'd been down there, but it sometimes seemed like forever. It was hard to remember a life on the outside. It was hard to remember the real world. Now it seemed that there was nothing but creeping on through the darkness, there was nothing but whispering and secrecy.

And in the darkness lay a man who was waiting to kill her . . .

UNDERWORLD II
"Tracey," she called quietly. No one answered. There was only the dark threatening void which forms Underworld. It's a place people can get lost in, people can disappear in. It's not a place for young girls whose big sisters have deserted them. Mandy didn't know what to do. She didn't know what had swept her sister and her friends from Underworld. All she knew was that Tracey had gone off and left her on her own.

UNDERWORLD III
Whose idea was it? Emma didn't know and now it didn't matter anyway. It was probably Adam who had said, "Let's go down and look round the Underground." It was something to tell their friends about, something new to try. To boast that they had been inside the secret Underworld, a place no one talked about, but everyone knew was there.

It had all seemed like a great adventure, until they found the gun . . .

Also by Peter Beere

CROSSFIRE
When Maggie runs away from Ireland, she finds herself roaming the streets of London destitute and alone. But Maggie has more to fear then the life of a runaway. Her step-father is an important member of the IRA – and if he doesn't find her before his enemies do, Maggie might just find herself caught up in the crossfire . . .